Our S...

~~200~~ Graham Road
South Windsor, CT 06074

SEASONS REMEMBERED

A TIME TO SEARCH

Linda Shands

≈
IVP

InterVarsity Press
Downers Grove, Illinois

InterVarsity Press® is the book-publishing division of InterVarsity Christian Fellowship®, a student movement active on campus at hundreds of universities, colleges and schools of nursing in the United States of America, and a member movement of the International Fellowship of Evangelical Students. For information about local and regional activities, write Public Relations Dept., InterVarsity Christian Fellowship, 6400 Schroeder Rd., P.O. Box 7895, Madison, WI 53707-7895.

Cover illustration: David Darrow
ISBN 0-8308-1933-9

Printed in the United States of America ∞

Library of Congress Cataloging-in-Publication Data

Shands, Linda, 1944-
    A time to search/Linda Shands.
        p.   cm.—(Seasons remembered)
    ISBN 0-8308-1933-9 (pbk.: alk. paper)
        1. Brothers and sisters—United States—Fiction.   2. Adoption—
    United States—Fiction.   I. Title.   II. Series: Shands, Linda,
    1944-   Seasons remembered.
    PS3569.H329T57   1995
    813'.54—dc20   *95-8897*
                                                                          CIP

| 17 | 16 | 15 | 14 | 13 | 12 | 11 | 10 | 9 | 8 | 7 | 6 | 5 | 4 | 3 | 2 | 1 |
| 09 | 08 | 07 | 06 | 05 | 04 | 03 | 02 | 01 | 00 | 99 | 98 | 97 | 96 | 95 |

To Gene
Thanks for your patience, encouragement
and support

Prologue

Echo Lake is calm today and mirror-smooth, except for a few ripples where a snow goose just landed.

Strange. The big brown and black honkers don't usually winter this far south. But then, strange things happen every day. Life takes twists and turns you'd never dream of.

There's a nip in the air that reminds me it's November. The park is almost empty except for a few mallards hunting crumbs along the shoreline. And the goose, of course. Papa would say that goose would look better dressed out on the Thanksgiving table, but Papa isn't here, and we'll most likely have the usual turkey with cranberries and stuffing this year.

I guess it's just as well Papa and Mama are gone. They'd never understand the graffiti painted on the wooden benches, or the rock 'n' roll music coming from inside the zoo. Libby says the animals like the music. "Especially the monkeys. You should see that old orangutan, Mom. He can dance just like Elvis."

Someone plastered a billboard picture of Marilyn Monroe on the plywood fence that guards the merry-go-round, now shut down for winter. They're making some repairs and repainting all the horses. The corral where they have the pony rides is empty too, except for the tall metal pole sticking straight up in the middle. Liberty Jane turned twelve last Fourth of July and hasn't ridden either of them in years. But she still likes the zoo. We come here often on Sunday afternoons.

Jake went in with her by himself today. "I'd just like to sit a while, if it's all right with you," I told them a few minutes ago.

Jake looked concerned, but then he saw the letters in my hand and smiled. "That's fine, babe. Take your time. We'll bring you a hot dog when we're through, won't we, sugar?"

"Daaad." Libby looked around to see if any of her friends were near. They weren't, of course, and Jake looked hurt for a moment.

I smiled at him, and he relaxed. "Sorry, Princess. I'll never call you sugar in public again, I promise." She rolled her eyes and marched off toward the ticket booth.

Jake shrugged. "Kids," I heard him mutter as he turned to follow.

I watched them go and shuffled the letters in my hand. I had read them a long time ago. But after all that had happened these past few years, I knew it was time to read them again. This time, maybe I would have a new perspective. This time, maybe I would feel less pain.

"Dear Celia," the first one began.

Or is it still Cissy? I never can remember what you go by now. You were Cissy for so long. I can remember when Papa named you that. You were such a little bitsy thing. The nickname seemed to suit you.

Those were such happy times! We didn't have much money, but your papa had a job. A good one too, as a clerk for the bank in Pike. Do you remember Nevada? Of course you do. You were eleven when we left, or was it ten? Oh dear. I guess it doesn't matter. You were old enough to know we'd lost the house and had to move.

You must understand, my precious girl, Papa only wanted the best for us. The whole country was suffering from the Depression. If he hadn't taken the money when he did, it would have all been lost anyway. I know that's no excuse, before God or man. But Papa repented of it after. Too late to save himself from prison and Roy Cummings's lying tongue, but soon enough to make amends with God.

I guess Roy got his revenge. On me and on your father. I used to cry and cry, curse Roy and wonder why losing our baby wasn't enough. Charles forgave me for that day with Roy. But you know that too. You guessed it all later when you were old enough to understand the way it is between a man and woman.

I never did ask you to forgive me, although my sin cost you everything you had: your home and family. Believe me when I say I know how you must have felt. I couldn't stand it myself. When they took your papa off to prison, I didn't want to live. I ran away, Celia, pure and simple, and left you to deal with it on your own. What a horrid thing for a mother to do!

The only way I knew to cope was to pretend. Pretty soon the pretending was more real than truth. It became my life. I didn't want to let you go. Not any of you. I knew you were too young to keep the family together, but I thought surely they would just appoint a guardian.

When they said they had a home for Chuck and the baby, I thought it would be for the best. Grace was so little, I knew she'd do fine. I didn't know about Chuckie. He relied so on you to tend to his needs. Even when we were still a family, it was you he preferred. And I was sick so much.

What choice did I have? He needed a mother, Celia. Surely you can understand that now. You have your precious Libby and that scamp of a husband, Jake. When I see you, you seem happy. I truly hope you are. I don't know about Chuck and Grace. I did the best I could at the time. I've written them too. These letters will all be together so that when I die you can read them and, I hope, understand.

I love you. If you believe nothing else, believe that. I've told Chuck and Grace the same. If you see them again, and I pray every day you will, give them each their letter. But not until they turn twenty-one. I want them to be old enough—to have lived long enough to understand.

I'm at peace, Celia. Believe that too. Kiss Libby for me, and my brother Edward. Tell Rose I can never repay her for what she did by taking you in. She truly is a saint, and I will see her in heaven.

God bless you, my darling daughter. I think I can rest now. Truly rest for the first time in years. Give my love to Jake and keep lots for yourself.

Love, Mama

Chapter One

Mama died in May of 1948, just three months before Libby's fourth birthday. The staff at Havenwood Manor were kind. They packed up all of Mama's things and had them waiting in the lobby when Aunt Rose, Libby and I went to collect them the day after the funeral.

I remembered the day they had transferred her there from the state hospital. It had looked so bright and open then, with polished floors and fresh-cut roses on a table by the door. Now, they had covered the floors with a garish red carpet and hung heavy gold drapes across the windows. The lobby held an oily smell, undercut with a hint of antiseptic. "They must have had fish for lunch," Aunt Rose whispered. It made my stomach curdle.

Mrs. Wentworth, who had the room next door to Mama's, met us by the entrance desk. She showed us a tatted doily Mama had made for her just weeks before she died.

"Mrs. Lynetta was a dear soul," she said and dabbed at her sightless eyes with a tissue from the wad she kept in her housecoat pocket. "She knew how I still love pretty things, even if I can't see my own hand before me. All I got to do is feel the stitches to know how lovely this is. Scalloped edges and all. I'll miss your mama, Celia dear. She made my life easier right up to the end."

I brushed my hand across my own damp cheeks and kissed her on the forehead. "Thank you, Mrs. Wentworth. Mama would be happy to know she helped someone."

"Liberty Jane, come away from that candy dish this instant!" Aunt Rose's scolding broke up the good-by scene. I took my errant daughter by the hand and hefted Mama's old carpetbag. Aunt Rose carried out the other two bags. They were feather light, she said. The sum of Mama's entire life, and it took up only half the back seat of the Chevy.

It was a while before I got around to sorting it. I was surprised at how clean and stylish the few pieces of clothing were. Her nightgown and bathrobe, though, were worn threadbare. The new ones Jake and I had given her for Christmas were still folded neatly in the box from Sears. In the end I kept a pair of slippers and a dressing gown I thought might suit Aunt Rose and gave the rest to charity.

I found my own keepsakes in the next two bags. Photographs—sorted and neatly labeled on the back with names and dates and places. Some were people I had never known, in places I had never been. Others were all too familiar and stirred a longing in my soul that I knew would never be satisfied.

I set the pictures aside. "I'll put them all in albums later," I promised the curious four-year-old peeping over my shoulder. "You can help me this winter. It will be a good project for a rainy day."

I tried to hide my emotions, but two tiny hands cupped my chin and turned my face toward her own. "Your eyes have puddles again, Mama. Are you sad?" She wrinkled her nose, and tears of sympathy formed in her blue eyes.

Mama's eyes. And Mama's frown. I caught her to my breast and held her close. Our reflection in the dressing-table mirror reminded me they were my eyes too. I realized then that no one ever really dies. They live on in those who come after them. And Mama's soul was waiting in heaven, with Papa and Krista and the baby she had lost so long ago.

"Mama! You're smovering me."

"Goodness, Libby, I'm sorry." I released my squirming daughter and kissed her cheek. She didn't brush the kiss away but searched my face intently, as if she were trying to find the right filling in a box of chocolate candy. I smiled at the thought. Libby's face relaxed, and she hopped off the bed.

"Gretel needs a bath," she announced and raced off to her room to fetch her beloved doll.

Libby had three dolls, but Gretel, made of a soft, squashy rubber, was her favorite. She could bathe, diaper and dress her "baby" like it was the real thing. Gretel was swaddled and petted, scolded and kissed, and rarely left her "mommy's" side.

I pushed the photographs to the back of the highest shelf in the linen closet and turned my attention to the third bag. Inside were two shoeboxes tied with string. The first still carried a thin layer of dust, as if it had been stored in an attic or under a bed. The second was clean and fairly new. I looked at the thick black lettering on the lid and realized it had held the slippers Libby had picked out for Mama's birthday last October. I found my paper scissors and cut the string.

I'd found a treasure.

There were more than a hundred in all. A legacy of letters to people she loved, both living and dead, filed neatly in chronological order. Mama had poured out her heart to a family that had been denied to her. The last was dated March 7, 1948, and addressed to Papa, as was the first, written in the wee hours of the morning on March 25, 1934, one week after Papa was arrested.

It took three days for me to get up the courage to read them.

Finally, on a moon-bright Friday night, after Libby was tucked in and Jake lay snoring softly with his pillow wadded up beneath his head, I slipped out of bed, grabbed a flashlight from the kitchen drawer and curled up on the back porch swing.

I began with those two, the first and the last, then filed all the rest of Papa's away. I thumbed through the missives to her mother, Grandma Eva, and her brother, Edward, and felt sick inside. But it was the ones she'd written just before she died— the ones addressed to Charles Byron Summers Jr. and Elizabeth Grace Summers—that tore my heart.

* * *

Aunt Rose pushed Libby on the swing, then wheeled my canvas clothes bag closer to the line. "Here, dear, hand me those pins, and I'll put them in the pocket for you."

I relinquished my handful of clothespins and folded another towel. "I have to find them, Aunt Rose. I know she said they weren't to have the letters until they're older, but I have to let them know she died."

I stacked the towels in the bottom of the fold-up bag and started on Jake's undershirts. "Besides, Chuckie's almost eighteen, and I'm sure he remembers. He was so scared when they took Mama away, and too little to understand. What has he been thinking all these years?"

"It won't be easy, sweetheart. You know your Uncle Edward's tried to find them more than once."

"I'll try again." I yanked the last shirt off the line and tossed it toward the bag. "He has a right to know she loved him!" I realized I was shouting and lowered my voice. "That's all Mama wanted. For them to know and someday understand."

Aunt Rose put her arms around my shaking shoulders and gave me a gentle squeeze. Then she pushed me to arm's length and studied my face. "Let's go in and sit awhile. I'll make us a pot of tea. How long since you slept through the night?"

I sighed, "It seems like forever." I picked up the shirt, laid it on top of the laundry cart and let Aunt Rose lead me toward the house. "Jake says if I don't sleep tonight he's going to drag me to the doctor kicking and screaming."

Aunt Rose turned around and called to Libby, "Play on your swing set, dear, and stay away from the incinerator. Mommy and I will be in the kitchen."

She led me to a chair and, within minutes, set two cups of steaming chamomile tea on the red Formica table. The cups were from the china set Mama had cherished so. That set of china was one of the few things that had been saved from the auction back in 1935. Mrs. Freeman had collected it before the sheriff locked the door and all Mama and Papa's possessions were sold to pay their debts.

"Jake's right," Aunt Rose said, interrupting my thoughts. "It's amazing what a good night's sleep will do." She sat down next to me and stirred some sugar into her tea. "I'll phone Mary Margaret and have her drop off a couple of her sleeping pills."

"I can't take pills. What if Libby wakes up?"

Aunt Rose smiled. "Jake can certainly tend to her if she needs something."

I wasn't convinced. Jake had never gotten up with Libby yet. "What could I do?" he always said. "She wants her mama."

Aunt Rose's smile faded, and her eyes shifted to the family portrait hanging on the dining-room wall. There were faces she didn't find there, and I knew she still felt the loss as well.

"I took sleeping pills for a week after your cousin Billy was killed in the war. That and prayer were the only things that kept me sane."

She sighed and took my hands in hers. I noticed how the veins puffed up and the tiny lines were etching ever deeper into the once-smooth skin. "God's grace is sufficient, sweetheart. Grief is a necessary thing, it heals. But he'll not leave you to grieve forever."

It sounded so easy. *But it isn't,* I thought, *especially now.*

The back door banged open, and Libby bounced into my just-scrubbed kitchen, flinging mud all over the service porch.

"Oh, my stars! Cissy, look at that child. And her new play dress!"

"Liberty Jane! What on earth—?" I echoed Aunt Rose's dismay at my daughter's mud-caked face and hair. Even Gretel was plastered from hairless head to naked toes with already-hardening brown mud.

Libby stopped stock-still and looked at us in wide-eyed innocence. Then she presented the naked Gretel for inspection. "We've just had a mud pack, see?" She cocked her head and clicked her tongue against the roof of her mouth. "When it dries," she instructed, "we'll wash it off and our skin will be soft and bootiful, just like Auntie M's."

Aunt Rose dissolved into helpless laughter.

"What's wrong with Nanna Rose?" Libby asked as I pulled the ruined jumper over her head.

I adjusted the faucets for warm water, then lifted her and Gretel into the laundry tub. "Nanna Rose is just tired, Libby."

I sighed as I sudsed up my daughter's auburn hair. Chuckie was just Libby's age when they took Mama away.

I'll find them, Mama, I vowed. *I swear I will.*

Chapter
Two

They were repaving Colorado Boulevard. I had to cross and walk two blocks down to Maple and another block back up to Vine. The breeze carried the suffocating smell of tar, and I felt like the thudding jackhammers were ripping through my head instead of the cement street.

I thought about Sister Veronica. I'd been surprised to find she was still the mother superior at St. Stephen's Orphanage. Only it wasn't an orphanage anymore. She hadn't been very encouraging when I'd phoned for an appointment. She was nice enough at first. "Of course I remember you, Celia," she'd said. "I'm not senile, you know. How have things worked out with your uncle?"

I assured her things had worked out fine and explained I was married now with a child of my own. Then I took a deep breath and got to the point.

"Mama died a few months ago. She left some letters. It's hard to explain on the phone, but I need to find Chuckie and Grace. May I come and talk to you?" She didn't answer right away. I could hear her intake of breath, and then a raspy wheezing filled the silence.

"Sister Veronica?"

"It won't do you any good to come here. I can't help you. I don't know where your brother and sister are." Her voice rose to a squeak, like a door hinge that needed oiling. "Even if I did know, I couldn't tell you."

It took three phone calls before she agreed to see me. She must have finally given in out of sheer exasperation. Maybe she thought she could convince me better in person that my quest was impossible.

I hadn't been to St. Stephen's in fifteen years. Not since December 1935, when Sister Anne, a novice then, had handed me a bag with my sweater and an extra dress in it and led me down the hall to Sister Veronica's office. They had been all smiles when Uncle Edward and Aunt Rose greeted me like they had known and loved me all my life. And I'm sure I saw a tear in Anne's eye when I turned to wave good-by.

Oak saplings had lined the street back then, like children waiting for a parade. Now they marched tall and stately, waving banners of yellow and orange leaves that sparked like fire in the afternoon sun. I would have enjoyed the spectacle if I hadn't been so anxious about the meeting.

The front porch looked the same. Broad thick steps led to the solid front door. The bell over the entry had rusted through, and the gong stayed silent when I pulled the chain. I wiped my sweaty palms with the hankie I'd tucked in the sleeve of my new blue suit, then reached for the knocker and banged it twice.

The sound echoed through the cavernous hall. I twisted the strap on my bag and reached to fluff my hair. The wind had blown it into a tangled mess, and I wished for the hundredth time I had the nerve to get it cut.

After an eternity, the door slid open. A slight young girl, who I guessed to be about nineteen, smiled at me shyly and stood aside for me to enter. *Anne?* I laughed nervously at the thought. Of course it wasn't Anne. She had no doubt moved on.

I followed the silent figure down the hall, past broad brown benches I had polished at least a dozen times. I still had the urge to tiptoe down the long gleaming floor until she turned, and our footsteps were muffled by a thick red carpet that led to the office door.

The girl held out her hand in an almost pleading gesture. "Please wait. I'll tell the Reverend Mother you're here."

The hall was as clean and sparse as I remembered it. A plain wooden table next to the door held a crucifix and what I took to be a prayer book. I smiled, remembering Sister Veronica's consternation when she discovered I wasn't "of the church." I never did learn all the prayers or how to use the rosary Sister Anne had given me. I hadn't been there long enough to try.

The pleasant smell of frying onions wafted from the kitchen. My stomach growled. I'd been too nervous to eat breakfast. Besides, I'd barely had time to get Libby dressed and fed, drop her off at Dotty's on the bus, and make my connection for Pasadena.

Jake is right, I thought. *I really must learn to drive.*

The door swung open. The young novice lowered her eyes and dipped her knees in a slight bow as she whispered, "The Reverend Mother will see you now."

Nothing about the office had changed. The same brown, scarred desk, water-stained blotter and stacks of paper piled neatly to the side. Volumes of books lined an entire wall. The windows, covered with the same heavy damask drapes, remained closed.

Sister Veronica sat unsmiling behind the desk, her hands folded serenely on the blotter. The sleeves of her robe fanned out, making her look like a hen protecting a brood of chicks.

"Celia." She nodded her greeting.

I stood in front of her, the child again, waiting to be instructed. It would never do to sit in the Reverend Mother's presence.

Not unless she gave permission.

I studied her face. She hadn't changed much except for a web of wrinkles that spread across her forehead to below her eyes and an extra fold of skin beneath her chin.

"It's not polite to stare. Or have you forgotten your manners?" I flushed, and she cleared her throat. "Now, tell me about this fool's errand. Why would you want to disrupt an entire family after all these years?"

I explained my need to see my brother and sister again, to tell them about Mama's death, to help them understand how much she loved them and why they were adopted.

I'd rehearsed the speech a hundred times in front of Jake, in front of the mirror, even in front of a wide-eyed Libby, who I'm sure understood as little as Sister Veronica did.

"They're grown now," I said lamely when she didn't respond. "I'm not trying to take them away from their family." I looked past her head to a plaster crucifix hanging on the wall and took a deep breath. "They were my family first. While I don't want to disrupt their lives, I do want to see them again. Surely you can understand that?"

I searched her face and thought I saw a flicker of sadness in her eyes, but when she spoke her voice was cool.

"Surely you can understand that you are being selfish. Don't you think they would try to find you if they were interested? I can assure you we've had no such inquiries from either of them."

"You can't send me away empty-handed."

"My dear child, I can do nothing else. Those records are sealed, and I'm afraid that's final. In any case, Mrs. Granger took them with her. Where they are, I would not presume to ask."

Her eyes flashed, then quickly softened. "You mustn't fight it, dear. The laws were made to protect adopted children and their families. I'm sure Charles and Grace have a good home, and it wouldn't be fair to torment their parents."

She stood with an effort, trying to stifle the small hissing sounds that escaped her throat with every breath. Her young helper appeared like a summoned ghost, and I knew the interview was over.

* * *

I stumbled to the bus stop in a daze. Air brakes whooshed as the bus pulled to the curb. I found a seat in back, between a man in greasy overalls and an elderly woman with a lap full of groceries.

What now? I hadn't expected to find them right off the bat. All I'd really hoped for was a scrap of information, just something to lead me in the right direction. I clutched my purse to keep my hands from shaking and tried to avoid the woman's curious stare. My feet throbbed, and suddenly I realized I'd stood throughout the whole ordeal.

I'd come all this way for nothing.

Chapter
Three

Aunt Rose always said, "The best way to get rid of anger is to work it off." And I'd lived with her long enough to know. By the time Jake came home that night, I could have served the pot roast on the kitchen floor and not picked up a germ.

I'd even baked two loaves of bread, but it turned out tough as nails. From beating the dough instead of kneading it, I guess. In the end, it had only served to dull my temper, not eliminate it.

If Jake noticed, he never said a word. He hung his greasy overalls on the nail just inside the back door and washed his hands with Lava soap at the kitchen sink. His job at Del Mar Transmission and Brakes was a good one, but he came home every night with wheel gunk on his hands. His fingernails were always stained with it.

I handed him a rag before he could ruin another dish towel, and he kissed me on the cheek. Not a real kiss. "A hen peck," Mama would have called it. But I was too mad to care.

"Jake," I waded right in, "you won't believe the way Sister Veronica treated me today! You'd have thought I was one of Satan's demons. Just because I want to see my brother and sister again."

Jake picked up the evening paper and settled in his place at the table. "What did you expect, Celia? I tried to tell you it wouldn't work. Those people never give anything away. Besides, the law says . . ."

"Daddy, Daddy!" Libby skidded into the room in stocking feet, dragging Gretel along by one arm. She was on his lap before he could set aside the paper and managed to crumple the entire sports section in the process.

"Liberty Jane, slow down! You'll upset the milk." I grabbed Jake's glass from under the ruined paper and moved it out of harm's way.

"How's my favorite little girl?" Jake crooned. He rubbed his stubbly chin against her cheek, which made her squeal in protest.

They were into their nightly routine, and I had to smile in spite of my mood. Jake and Libby. They were my world. Yet part of me still longed after Mama and Papa. And Chuck and Grace too, of course. No one could ever convince me that we wouldn't have been better off if they'd just kept us together. I had helped Mama with everything from diapers to dishes; I could certainly have managed my brother and sister just fine.

After dinner, Jake and I tucked Libby into bed and heard her prayers. Jake settled into his easy chair with a *Popular Science* magazine, and I took up the sweater I was knitting for Dotty and Sam's third baby. It was only September and the baby wasn't due until January, but Dotty was big as a house already.

She had called me just last night almost in tears.

"Oh, Celia, that doctor is impossible," she moaned. "When he checked the baby's heartbeat, he frowned and tapped the stethoscope with his finger. Then he muttered, 'Could be an echo,' and patted me on the tummy like he would a puppy dog." I could hear the fear underneath the indignation in her voice.

"I asked if anything was wrong, but he just said, 'No, no, my dear, nothing to worry your pretty head about. We'll sort it out. Now you make sure and get plenty of rest, and you might skip a dessert or two.' And he laughed, like he thought he was Bob Hope or something.

"Can you imagine, Celia? How can I rest? Rachel's into everything at once, and David howls every time I set him on the potty chair. Besides, I can't keep down a bowl of oatmeal, let alone dessert!"

I had tried to reassure her, but privately I wondered what they were thinking. Three babies in just over four years! It made me tired just to think of it. But that was their choice. I had problems of my own.

I sighed and let myself relax with the rhythm of my work. Knit one, purl two; the needles clicked, soothing the turmoil in my mind until I realized I was hearing a name with every other beat. *Mrs. Granger . . . Mrs. Granger . . . Mrs. Granger.*

"Mrs. Granger!" I dropped the half-done sweater into the bag at my feet and sat forward on the couch. "Jake. The social worker's last name was Granger. Sister Veronica as much as told me so."

Jake scowled at me over the top of his magazine. "Are you still stewing about this adoption thing? I thought we'd settled that. This Mrs. Ranger or whatever her name is won't tell you any more than you already know."

I bit my lip to keep from answering back. Jake wouldn't like what I had to say, and I knew I'd be just as sorry later for saying it.

After several minutes of quiet, I looked up and said, "I'm going to bed." I forced myself to walk over for a good-night kiss. Jake dutifully pecked my cheek and went back to his magazine.

Later, when I had finally calmed down enough to sleep, I felt him slide into bed and gather me into his arms. "I'm sorry, babe. I know this means a lot to you." He pulled my head against his chest and ran his fingers through my hair. Shades of brown had slowly overcome the brilliant gold, but I was still young enough to wear it past my shoulders, and I had let it grow. For Jake.

"I'll help you any way I can. But I'm afraid you'll just get hurt again." He tipped my chin and handed me his hankie from the dresser by the bed. "The records are sealed, Cissy girl. You need a court order to open them. That takes good cause and a sympathetic judge."

"Mama's dead. They're my family, and they need to know."

I could feel his head shake in the darkness. "It's not enough, babe. It would take a medical emergency, maybe. But there's nothing like that going on."

In my mind I knew he was right, but in my heart I knew I had to try.

* * *

I spent most of the next week on the phone and finally located Mrs. Granger at a private adoption agency in Canoga Park. I gathered my courage and, in spite of Jake's warnings, had Uncle Edward drive me over.

It was a clear, sun-drenched October day. The breeze nipped my ears with a hint of cooler weather, and the maple trees had just begun to pepper the ground with red and orange leaves. I held my head high and gathered hope around me like a shield.

Mrs. Granger wore a dark-blue woolen suit and a creamy yellow blouse with an old-fashioned button-up collar. Her graying hair was done up in a bun, and when she came around from behind her desk, I noticed she wore sensible, low-heeled shoes. I would not have known her.

It was obvious she didn't remember me either. She must have thought I was a potential client as she smiled and offered me a seat. My legs were Jell-O, and I sat down gratefully on the stiff leather sofa across from her desk. It was the only other piece of furniture in the room, and I had to perch on the edge to keep myself from sliding into the crack between the cushions.

"I need to find my family," I began. "Their names are Charles Byron and Elizabeth Grace Summers. They'd be seventeen and thirteen now. And if it helps, I believe the couple who took them in were well-to-do."

Her smile had faded after the first six words. By the time I got to the point, her face was livid.

"Stop right there, young woman, I've heard enough!" She slapped her hands on the desk and stood, upsetting a potted plant and scattering soil all over the light green rug. "You have some nerve coming in here, trying to trick me into giving out privileged information."

"But . . ." I hated the quiver in my voice, but her violent reaction took me by surprise.

"I will not be a party to trickery. Those people have a right to privacy, and you'll get no answers from me." She stepped around the desk and pointed to the door. "I think you had better leave."

* * *

"That hateful woman!" I complained to Uncle Edward. "What can I do now?"

Uncle Edward shook his head. "I don't know, sweetheart. We'll think of something." What he didn't say was that he'd tried before and gotten nowhere either.

Jake tried to be sympathetic, but I knew he was thinking, *I told you so.*

I tried several more times to see Mrs. Granger, but she wouldn't even accept my phone calls. By December I knew I had failed.

Chapter
Four

I spent the weeks before Christmas prowling the stores, searching out the perfect gifts for Libby and Jake. I walked on dry white sidewalks under palm trees that fanned an April-warm breeze. I wondered if I would I ever get used to the weather in Southern California.

Back in Pike we'd be sloshing through a foot of snow, bundled up in jackets and fur-lined rubber boots. Papa would take his ax and fell the perfect tree in the woods up by Humble Mountain. He'd bring home an armload of cedar branches to line the mantle and make pine-cone wreaths for all the neighbors. But he always saved the prettiest for our own front door. The fragrant fir and cedar always filled the wood-frame house, competing with the aroma of pumpkin pies and cranberry muffins wafting from Mama's kitchen. I smiled when I rounded the corner onto Main Street in Alhambra and felt a slight chill to the wind that tugged at my old beige sweater.

Christmas shopping was a pleasant chore I usually shared with Dot, but this year she was confined to bed. Her child seemed determined to birth early.

In my opinion that was just as well.

"If she gets any bigger, her belly will pop," I had told Jake the night before.

He chuckled and set aside the evening paper. "I would bet a dollar she's hatching more than one." He shook his head. "Poor Sam."

"What do you mean, 'poor Sam'? And Dotty's a mother, not a chicken!" I'd been filling dishes with nuts and ribbon candy. I grabbed a huge black walnut and pitched it at Jake. It hit him hard, right between the eyes.

"Ow!" He grinned and rubbed the red mark on his forehead. "I knew I'd rue the day Billy taught you how to throw."

I grinned back. My cousin Billy had been only ten when I went to live with Aunt Rose and Uncle Edward, but he could sure play baseball. Jake was no slouch at the game either. Between the two of them I'd developed a pretty good arm myself.

"Anyway, with the baby, or babies," I conceded, "so close to coming, I told Dotty I'd do her shopping too. Who knows, she may be in the hospital on Christmas Day."

"Like your mother was with Chuck."

His face turned red, and I knew he was sorry the instant he said it. I let it pass. I'd been thinking the same thing.

Chuckie would be eighteen this year. I couldn't help but wonder where he was. How would he celebrate his birthday? Would they have a party or let it go because of Christmas? There were so many questions I might never find the answers to. I constantly found myself searching the crowds of Christmas shoppers for a tall young man with dark blond curls and a five-year-old's face.

I discovered the rocking horse Libby wanted at a secondhand store on Garfield Boulevard. It was made of wood and leather and looked like something Papa would have ridden as a boy. "Real horsehair for the mane and tail," the salesman bragged. "None of this plastic stuff with springs. They don't make them like this anymore."

I nodded and reluctantly handed over a ten-dollar bill, enough to buy groceries for a week. Libby had insisted this horse was all she wanted, and Jake had insisted we get it.

"We'll spoil her, Jake," I'd protested.

"So what? We're not like Sam and Dot; we only have one child. Why not spoil her a little?" He turned away, and I knew the discussion was over.

Neither of us liked to talk about the other baby, the one I'd lost almost before we knew I was expecting. The doctor had assured us all was well. "You can have ten more if you want, Mrs. Freeman," he had joked. But no more babies had come along, and now Libby was over four years old.

It was a good thing I'd finished my shopping early. Aunt Rose called to ask if I'd bring pies for Christmas dinner. I had just hung up the phone when it rang again.

"Celia? I've got to get Dot to the hospital. She says we don't have time to drop off the kids. Can you come?"

Sam sounded like he'd just run the Kentucky Derby. His words came out on short puffs of air and ended in a high-pitched whinny. "Eegads! Dotty, don't push, I'll be right there. Celia, the kids are asleep in David's crib. I put the side up so they can't get out. Hurry."

The line went dead.

"Oh, grief. Jake, watch Libby. I have to get to Dotty's now!" I grabbed my sweater from the back of the dining-room chair and raced out the door. I'd gone three blocks before I remembered two things: I'd never been able to run an inch without my legs turning into rubber bands, and if I'd only had my head on straight, I could have asked Jake to drive me. But I was too close to turn back now. What could Sam be thinking? Those little monkeys could have the house down around their ears in one second flat, crib or no crib.

By the time I limped into the living room I had conjured up

all sorts of nasty surprises, from cuts and bruises to blood and fire. Instead the house was quiet. Deathly quiet. I stumbled through the hallway into the postage-stamp bedroom and tip-toed over to the crib.

David looked like an angel in his fuzzy white sleeper. He was curled up at one end of the crib, his thumb and the edge of a ragged blanket tucked firmly in his mouth.

Rachel was nowhere to be seen.

"Rachel?" I whispered as loudly as I could. "Rachel, where are you? Come see Aunt Celia."

In the silence, I realized my heart was still pounding, and I hadn't caught my breath from my five-block run. I moved away from the crib and stumbled into the rocking chair. My rubber-legs buckled, and I landed bottom down on the hard, wooden seat.

"Oh, grief!"

David's eyes popped open, and he grinned at me, an elfin grin that fit his impish personality to a tee. At the same time I heard a high-pitched giggle and saw the closet door swing wide. A laughing bundle of flannel nightgown and silk-brown hair launched herself into my lap.

"Rachel Hanna Levi, you scared me to death." I tickled her ribs and she squirmed into a comfortable position, her rear against my stomach, head thrown back against my chest. "Read me?" She wheedled and handed me a cloth-bound copy of *The Night Before Christmas.*

Before I could recover enough to answer her, I heard a car door slam. An instant later, Jake stood in the doorway, our daughter in his arms. He looked from the crib to the rocker and back again, then set Libby on the floor. He was almost as out of breath as I had been a moment ago. "Woman, don't ever do that to me again." He sat down on his haunches, shook his head and began to laugh.

* * *

Sarah Lynn and Jacob Joseph Levi were born ten minutes apart, with tiny Sarah leading the way at five pounds, fourteen ounces. Jacob topped the scales at exactly six pounds. In the years to come, he would never let anyone forget he was the bigger, if not the older, of the pair.

Sam came to our house for dinner that night. "I swear I thought we'd never make it." He pushed his plate away and began to rub the muscles in his thighs. "I had to help lift her to the gurney, and I was sure she'd deliver in the parking lot." He grinned and shifted his weight to the other hip.

"How about that, huh? One more of each. My quiver is truly full." He sighed and pushed to his feet. He grimaced, but did not complain as he walked slowly around the room.

My heart thumped as it always did when I watched Sam walk, and I thanked God for the miracle that had let it happen. It had been eight years since the hit-and-run that had left him crippled—an "accident" that had been arranged for me by the same men who had framed my father for murder.

I had long since given up feeling guilty about Sam's physical condition, but I had to admit that the return of feeling to his legs and the surgery that allowed him to walk again had helped to heal my broken spirit as well.

"Would you like to stay over too?" I asked as I helped him tuck Rachel into Libby's bed. "I could make up the couch."

"No. Thanks, Celia, but I have court in the morning. A murder case, and I'm the prosecutor." He reached over the railing on Libby's old crib and pulled the blanket up to David's chin. "I'm glad it's just the preliminaries; I'm too excited to sleep. I have a feeling it's going to be a long night." He kissed me good-night and shook Jake's hand.

Jake threw an arm around Sam's shoulder. "Congratulations, buddy. You better rest while you can. You'll be working seven

A Time to Search

days a week to support this bunch."

Sam grinned and made his way slowly down the porch steps
to his new Packard Super 8 convertible. It was a dream of a
car: yellow with whitewall tires. He'd ordered it fitted with
special blocks on the pedals so he wouldn't have to exert too
much pressure on his leg muscles when he drove.

As we watched the car disappear around the corner, I felt
Jake's arms come around my waist. He pulled me close and held
me. His heart beat steady against my cheek, his warm breath
ruffling my hair, and I thought I could have stayed right there
forever.

Chapter
Five

In the spring of 1949, Jake and I bought a doll house in San
Gabriel, a quiet suburb eight miles east of Los Angeles. The
house was brand-new, finished with a cream-colored stucco. It
had a covered, cement front porch, not nearly as big as the ones
I'd grown up with, but the tall wooden lattice between the
living-room and bedroom windows made up for it. We hadn't
been there a week before I planted roses. By the end of summer
they had climbed almost to the eaves.

The entire house would have fit inside Aunt Rose's downstairs. But like Jake pointed out, we only needed two bedrooms
and one bath. The living room had an archway that opened into
a dining room, and a swinging door blocked off the kitchen. The
whole thing suited us just fine.

Aunt Rose had given her extras to Mary Margaret, so we
bought new furniture, Venetian blinds and new white sheers.
I had to press the ruffles on the curtains, and they snagged
easily, but they were identical to the ones Mama used to have
in our living room on York Street. It made me feel as if I had
a small part of her with me.

I was still trying to find Chuckie and Grace, but no one with
the authority to help would give me the time of day. The clerk

at the hall of records shook his head. "Not without a court order," he said. "If you're wise, young woman, you'll leave it alone."

In May, I persuaded Sam to file a petition with the court.

"I'll do it, Celia, but I have to tell you I don't think you have much chance. They're pretty cut and dried about these things."

It turned out he was right. The judge looked at me like I was a home wrecker and banged his gavel on the desk. "You don't show good cause," he growled, "and you're wasting the court's time."

I closed my eyes and thought of Mrs. Granger. I saw her angry face and heard her ugly words: "I will not be a party to trickery. Those people have a right to privacy, and you'll get no answers from me."

Sister Veronica had come right out and called me selfish: "You're on a fool's errand," she had said.

I decided Jake and the others were right. I would never find my family this way. And I just couldn't take any more of the hurt.

Not that I ever gave up looking, or praying. Whenever we went to the fair or the beach—anywhere crowds of people gathered—I watched for familiar faces: a teenager who looked like Krista with her red-gold curls or a young man with Papa's smile. Once I saw a girl at the beach who looked so much like Krista grown it took my breath away. But it turned out not to be.

"No, ma'am," she said, shaking her head politely. "My name is Florence, Florence DuVal. That's my mom over there."

She pointed to a tiny wisp of a woman in an expensive Catalina swimsuit. She was propped on one elbow, slender fingers tracing patterns in the sand, watching her daughter and me with a worried frown.

Just as I'd decided to let it go, a tall man who looked to be a few years younger than Uncle Edward sprinted across the sand. Shaking water from his hair and eyes, he draped one arm across the girl's shoulders and ruffled her hair. "Hey, Pumpkin, what's going on?"

The girl grinned up at him with obvious pleasure. "This is my father," she said without even glancing back at me. "It's okay, Dad. This lady had me mixed up with someone else."

I smiled my apology and turned away. I could see Jake and Libby coming back from the refreshment stand trying to balance hot dogs and Cokes for three. Libby was carrying her bathing cap and towel as well, and hopping from one foot to the other in the hot sand. I ran to help them, and when we returned to our blanket, the girl and her family had gone. I kept the encounter to myself. No one else would have understood.

Not even Jake. He still had most of his family and his old home to go back to now and then. Tim was gone, of course. Like Billy, he'd been killed in action during the war. Jake's sister Anne had married a man named Frank Spellman, a doctor she had served with in the Philippines. After the war they had moved to San Francisco. They came for visits when they could, but the doctor wasn't well. A recurring case of malaria kept him housebound most of the time. The others all lived at home, although Sara June had found a sweetheart and was talking about a spring wedding. John and Brian were still in high school, and the twins, at twelve, kept things hopping. Davy especially was a handful, and he pretty much ran his parents ragged. Jake had to go over there every so often and "settle his bacon," as Ma Freeman said.

* * *

In the fall of 1950, Libby started first grade at The Master's Christian Day School. Jake and I had joined First Baptist Church with Dotty and Sam, and it seemed best to send the children to school there.

The school wasn't in the church but in a twelve-room building next to it. They had turned one of the parking lots into a large playground, with swings and monkey bars and room for jumprope and dodgeball. The teachers were friendly and, as Mrs. Morrison, the principal, assured me, well qualified.

"You'll find the curriculum here a bit more advanced than public schools," she confided, "but your Libby did well on her readiness tests. She should manage just fine."

"Do you think we did the right thing?" I asked Jake after the first week of school. "Libby's bright and eager to learn, but I don't want her to feel overwhelmed. I think they expect too much of the students there."

"Nonsense. It won't hurt her to work. It'll do her good to be pushed a little." Jake sounded for all the world like Papa when he talked like that.

"I don't mean her studies. She's already reading better than most of her classmates."

"Then what are you talking about, woman?" He set his paper aside with exaggerated patience and handed me his coffee cup. I filled it from the pot on the stove and poured myself a second cup of tea.

"Well, I've already had a phone call from Mrs. Woodbridge." Jake looked blank. "Libby's teacher. Honestly, you never have any trouble remembering baseball scores." I went on before he could answer back. "Libby's already in trouble for bossing some of the younger children. She was supposed to be reading out loud from the primer, when she stopped in the middle of a sentence and told Billy Martin to get his thumb out of his mouth or she wouldn't finish the story."

Jake couldn't stop the laughter that shook the table and spilled coffee into his saucer. I took a sip of tea to keep from chuckling myself. "Well, the teacher didn't think it was so funny. Libby embarrassed Billy in front of the whole class." I sighed. "I think Mrs. Woodbridge understood when I explained that Libby's used to bossing David and the twins.

"In any case, I guess she reprimanded Libby quite soundly and made her apologize to Billy. Then she let him finish reading the story. Libby was humiliated and sulked all afternoon. I'm not sure I know what to do about it."

"Do? There's nothing to do, Celia. It sounds to me like the teacher handled it. Libby will be fine." Jake was still smiling as he mopped the bottom of his cup with a dishrag. "If that's all the trouble she ever gets into, we can count ourselves blessed."

* * *

When Libby was in second grade, Sam and Dotty enrolled Rachel at the school. David joined them a year later, but not before Dotty had another baby.

Ezekiel Aharah Levi fought his way into the world on a dreary, rain-drenched morning in January 1951. Dotty had a time of it, to say the least, and we were all relieved when the husky, dark-eyed baby took his allotted place in the hospital nursery.

"Ezekiel Aharah?" Jake said to Sam as we stood gazing through the window at the row of blanket-bound infants. "What made you choose a name like that?"

I jabbed my elbow into Jake's ribs, but Sam didn't seem to mind the question. "Ezekiel means 'God strengthens.' " He chuckled and wiggled his fingers at his sleeping son. "Aharah means 'comes after' or 'last,' and Dot has assured me in no uncertain terms that this one is the last.

"We'll call him Zeke." He said it as an afterthought, and from then on Ezekiel Aharah became just plain Zeke.

By the end of January, Dotty had already settled into her old routine. I don't know how she did it, but five children didn't seem to faze her. "After three, it can't get any worse," she assured me. "In fact, Rachel and David are a big help with the twins and little Zeke. I just don't want to go through it again." She shivered. "I thought it was supposed to get easier, but this one was harder than Rachel. Anyway, I'm getting too old to have babies."

* * *

Sam's law practice was thriving, and in the fall of 1952 he and Dotty bought a house in Temple City. The house was huge, hacienda style with black wrought-iron railings, a tree-shaded patio and a kidney-shaped swimming pool. It had four bedrooms and two baths upstairs, an enormous living room, a formal dining room and a den. There was even what Dotty called a "half-bath" between the kitchen and the laundry room.

By that time Jake had earned another promotion and another raise. He was now the top mechanic at Del Mar Transmission and Brakes, but we still didn't make the kind of money Sam brought home.

It didn't matter, though. Truth to tell, I loved my home and wouldn't have traded it for a thousand of Dotty's. With five children, she and Sam needed all the room they could get. And the big back yard was practically a necessity in the summer when she had to keep them all entertained. Jake wasn't envious either. At least if he was he didn't show it.

Besides, their lives weren't any more perfect than ours were. Sam experienced constant leg pain. When his muscles went into spasm, he could barely function. Jake mowed the grass for him and did other chores that required more strength than Sam had to give. In turn, Sam loaned Jake money when we needed a new car. And in the summer of 1953, he gave us free legal advice when some neighbors threatened to sue us over a torn-up lawn.

The Fergusons, an older couple who seemed fairly well-to-do, had moved into the house on the corner right after Easter.

"I can't imagine why they'd want to move into a neighborhood like this," I told Jake one Saturday in May. We were transplanting a camellia bush in the side yard next to the porch, and we could see Mr. Ferguson out watering his new dichondra lawn.

"Why not?" Jake straightened up and called hello to the Miller boys, who were racing their bikes up and down the street.

"For one thing, they don't have any kids." I waved my arm to point out a group of children playing ball in the street and the Keller girls rolling down the sidewalk, skate keys bouncing against their chests.

"And," I continued, "they're certainly not interested in being neighborly. I took a coffee cake over the other day, and she was positively rude. 'We don't eat sweets, and my husband isn't one for company,' she said and closed the door right in my face."

Jake finished patting down the soil around the bush. "Well, just leave them alone then. Not every neighbor needs to be a lifelong friend."

"At least they could be nice." I held the gate for him to push the wheelbarrow through.

Our cocker spaniel, Jingles, slipped out before I could get it latched again.

"Celia," Jake hollered, "catch that dog before he runs off! I don't want to chase him all over the neighborhood."

I got down on my haunches and wiggled my fingers like I had a cookie or a piece of wiener. Jingles was the least intelligent dog I'd ever met, but he would do almost anything for food. "Come on, boy," I crooned. "Come see what Mommy's got for you."

I almost had him. But just as I grabbed for his collar, Libby and Rachel came racing around the corner with David in hot pursuit. Even from where I sat, I could see that the object of their terror was a long, black garden racer that David held out in front of him like a sword. He and the snake had almost caught up with his squealing victims when Jingles caught sight of Libby and bolted away to join the fun.

I scrambled to my feet and yelled, "Watch out!"

Jingles launched himself at Libby, knocking her sideways into Rachel. David slipped on the wet sidewalk and went sprawling. Before I could get my wits about me, dog, kids, and snake collided into a yowling, squirming heap in the middle of the Ferguson's dichondra.

Jake came back through the gate and had just started toward the corner to help untangle the mess, when Mr. Ferguson, red faced and yelling obscenities, turned the hose on all of them.

Jingles didn't need another invitation to leave. The only thing he hated worse than fleas was water. He dug in his back feet and, kicking up a divot that would embarrass even the worst weekend golfer, launched himself back to the sidewalk and off to kingdom come.

Libby and Rachel had somehow landed on top of David and caused him to loose his grip on the snake, which had the utmost desire to be gone as well.

Now, I don't pretend to understand the snake's motives, but I swear it calculated all the risks and decided the best place for a serpent right then was under the Ferguson's porch. Unfortunately, Mrs. Ferguson had followed her husband out onto the lawn and the only snake-size route was between her feet.

I never saw a woman dance like that before or since. She hopped from one foot to the other like a soul possessed, churning up soil faster than a herd of rampaging buffalo.

By the time the children had sorted themselves out and Mrs. Ferguson had landed on her bottom in the mud, the whole dichondra patch looked like it had been plowed for planting, and Jake was nose to nose with Mr. Ferguson.

The exchange that followed was not fit for tender ears. I shooed all three children toward our yard and, after making sure Mrs. Ferguson didn't need a doctor, dragged them inside the house. Jake came home fifteen minutes later. While he drove Rachel and David home, I tried to explain to Libby why I couldn't wash her father's mouth out with soap.

Jake was as testy as a hornet for two whole days. Finally, on Wednesday, right after the evening news, he clicked off the TV and headed out the door.

"I have to go down there and apologize," he said when I asked where he was going. "I won't have any peace until I do."

When he came back, his face was red and his eyes snapped fire. "You can't say I didn't try," was all he said.

A few days later a man in an off-white Cadillac pulled up in front and served Jake with a summons. Sam defended us, and the judge threw the case out of court.

Chapter
Six

Poor Jingles never did come home. Libby was heartbroken for a week. "He's out there all alone," she sobbed. "I just know he's hungry and scared."

I finally crossed my fingers behind my back and told her, "I'm sure he's found another home. Why, someone is probably cutting up hot dogs for his dinner right this minute." I fervently hoped that was true.

What I didn't tell Libby was that, for Jingles, running away was a far better fate than what her father had planned for him. "Good riddance," was all Jake had to say on the subject. He refused even to check the pound.

After a while, Libby quit fussing about the loss of her dog. She and Rachel were inseparable, and Libby spent more time at Sam and Dotty's than she did at home.

On the few occasions when we had to separate the two girls, they sulked like pups in a kennel. We kept them apart for two weeks after Rachel got the chicken pox. But when Libby sprouted blisters ten days later, we decided it was a hopeless cause.

"Let it make the rounds," Dotty sighed in resignation. "They all have to get them sometime; it might as well be now."

The trouble was, the twins broke out over Christmas vacation and Dotty really had her hands full. I wound up taking Rachel and David, along with Libby, out to Aunt Rose's for a week. The kids bundled up every morning for a romp in the chill country air, while Aunt Rose and I made pies, polished silver and wrapped presents to our hearts' content.

"You're an angel, Cissy girl." Dotty hugged me when I dropped the kids off on my way home to pick up Jake on Christmas Eve. "You can't imagine how much I got done with them away."

She dabbed calamine on Sarah and Jacob Joe's scabbed-over legs and set the bottle on the sink. Then she scooped up little Zeke, plopped him in the high chair and handed him a crayon and a piece of newspaper to scribble on. For being the baby of the bunch, Ezekiel was remarkably unspoiled. He was good-natured, easy to please, and I never once saw him throw a temper tantrum.

"Why should he?" Jake said when I commented on the almost two-year-old's restraint. "The whole bunch caters to his every whim. What's he got to complain about?"

"You should talk. You cart him around like a pony every time we're over there. And don't think we don't see you slip him Life Savers when the other kids aren't looking!"

Jake opened his eyes wide in feigned innocence. "Who, me?" he protested and busied himself arranging packages in the trunk of the car. He lowered the trunk lid and locked it. "All set. Are you ready, Celia? I'm hungry, and my taster's set for a piece of Rosebud's apple pie."

The change in subject matter couldn't fool me. I knew the affection Jake felt for Zeke. But I felt a twinge of sadness as I shook out my umbrella and climbed into the car for the trip back to San Bernardino. I wondered, as I had a thousand times, if the child we'd lost had been a boy or a girl. Jake had so wanted a son.

I studied my husband's profile as he switched on the windshield wipers and pulled out onto the street. I would never get over feeling there was an empty place in our family. I knew it was wrong to question God, but I couldn't understand why he had chosen to give us only one child. Not that we weren't grateful for Libby. She was the light of my life and her father's pride and joy. But we both felt there was room in our hearts and home for several more.

I tried not to dwell on it, but there were times, like now, when I actually ached with longing for Chuckie and Grace. Never mind that they'd be grown by now. They would always be babies to me.

* * *

In spite of all Aunt Rose and I had already done, there was still the tree to decorate and cooking to do. We tucked Libby in Billy's old twin bed and made up the roll-away for Mary Margaret. Jake and I had volunteered to keep Libby with us, but my cousin wouldn't hear of it.

"I don't get to see her near enough as it is, Celia. She's only my second cousin, but she's like a niece to me, and I should think you'd want me to get to know her."

I rolled my eyes and let it be. It didn't matter that we were just concerned for Mary Margaret's comfort. She was determined as always to play the martyr.

Her divorce from Wesley had been final for some time. She had given up and quit fighting in the end, but had built a wall around the wound of rejection and refused to let anyone in. I'm sure she must have grieved in private, but in public she played the part of a gay, carefree divorcée to the hilt. To family, though, her preferred role was one of long-sufferance mixed with a generous helping of self-pity. It could be tiresome.

Still, it could have turned out to be one of the nicest Christmases we had had. Libby was a fairly easygoing nine-year-old, and she was devoted to her Auntie M. And with Libby, Mary Margaret didn't need a façade. Our daughter brought out the child in her, and I came to realize that was exactly what my cousin wanted: to be a child again, free from the pressures and pain of an adult world.

* * *

Christmas fell on Monday that year, so they had the entire weekend to entertain each other. In fact, Jake and I had so much free time, we even took a walk after church on Christmas Eve. We strolled through the village and on past my old school, Central High. We ignored the torn-down archway and the graffiti that soiled the low brick wall, and concentrated on the elaborate display of lights in the neighborhood.

In one yard a huge cardboard Santa held the reins to a wrought-iron sleigh. In another, fake reindeer danced across a floodlighted roof. I was disappointed that there were no manger scenes, until we rounded the corner back onto Sherwood Lane and noticed a small crowd of people gathered at the vacant lot where Billy and I used to play ball. "Look, Jake, something's going on." I grabbed his arm, and we moved toward the field. Someone had organized a tableau with Mary and Joseph, wise men and shepherds, a donkey and a lamb. Baby Jesus lay on a bed of straw piled in a wooden egg crate. A record player set up behind the makeshift barn played "Silent Night" and "Away in the Manger."

The baby cried. As we watched, Mary moved from Joseph's side, picked up the infant and cradled him tenderly. Before we could blink, it seemed the whole neighborhood had gathered. Someone in the group began to sing. We added our voices, and it seemed the very stars echoed the words: "Joy to the world, the Lord has come ..."

"Merry Christmas, darling." Jake smiled and tucked my arm

through his as we turned toward home.

We hadn't been back to the house three minutes when the phone rang.

"Jake, it's for you." Mary Margaret's eyebrows met the wrinkles in her forehead. "It's your mother, and she sounds upset."

Jake scowled and took the receiver. "Ma?" He listened for a minute, then shut his eyes and sat down on a dining-room chair.

I pulled out a chair and sat next to him, but he wouldn't look at me.

"Is she coming home?" Another pause. "All right, we'll call you later." He cradled the receiver and sat with his head down for the longest time.

Finally I couldn't stand it any longer. "Jake, please, you're scaring me. What's wrong?"

He grabbed my hand and held on. "It's Anne Marie. Frank had another attack of malaria. Only this time he didn't pull through. He died this morning."

"Oh, no! Poor Anne. Where is she? Do we need to go and get her?"

"She's at home. Ma and Pa offered to go up, but she asked them not to." Jake let go of my hand and accepted Aunt Rose's arm around his shoulder.

"What can we do, dear? If you need help getting to the funeral . . ."

Jake stood and moved toward the window. "Evidently Frank had requested that there be no funeral. Just a memorial service at their church. Ma said it's scheduled for Tuesday, and Anne told her not to come. It's too far to drive all the way to San Francisco for such a short time."

"But Jake, shouldn't someone be there?" I asked. "I mean, Anne shouldn't be alone at a time like this."

Jake shrugged. "What can I do, Celia? She told Ma not to let anyone come." He unrolled his shirtsleeves and plucked his jacket from the rack by the front door. "I'm going out awhile. When I get back, we'll call her ourselves, okay?" He kissed me on the cheek and left.

It turned out to be a solemn evening. Even Libby was subdued. "Did I know him, Mom?" she asked when I tucked her into bed that night.

I nodded. "I think you met him twice, but it's been awhile. We don't expect you to remember." That seemed to soothe her.

"I'll pray for Aunt Anne before I go to sleep," Libby promised.

"You do that." I stroked her hair back off her forehead and kissed the fuzzy spot just below the hairline. "Anne will need all of our prayers in the next few weeks."

* * *

I helped Aunt Rose set gifts under the tree and fill the crocheted stockings we'd hung from hooks above the hearth. None of us had much to say. We were all remembering other loved ones lost to that evil monster, Death. There had been too many for one family. Far too many.

My heart ached for Anne Marie.

Chapter
Seven

I have never forgotten the newsreel that brought to life the sheer horror of the atomic bomb that devoured Hiroshima in 1945. The scene held us spellbound by its awesome power and the awful realization of its possibilities.

I winced at the silent explosion. Every eye in the theater was riveted to the screen as the gray mushroom cloud billowed upward, growing taller and wider by the second. Then the scene changed and we were drawn, open-mouthed and gasping, to the mayhem and destruction on the ground below. Jake sat stiff as stone, his mouth set in a straight, hard line. I didn't try to stem the tears that coursed silently down my cheeks.

There was a smattering of applause. Didn't they know any better? One tiny atom, in one split second, had changed the world. Life would never be the same again.

* * *

It was July 1955, two years after the passing of Annie's Frank and a full ten years after Hiroshima, when the phone rang after midnight. In later years that sound would fill me with dread. But in those days Mary Margaret still worked the graveyard shift, and once in a while she'd forget about the hour and call us anyway. So when Jake groaned and rolled over, I mumbled, "I'll get it," and stumbled into the dining room.

"Celia!" Mary Margaret shouted. "It's Daddy. Mama said we'd all better come. Can you and Jake pick me up?"

I felt the blood rush to my head and gripped the table to steady myself. "Slow down, I can't understand you. What's wrong with Uncle Edward?"

"Oh, Celia," she started to sob, "Mama just called. There's been an accident, and Daddy's in the hospital. Mission Valley, I think she said, just this side of San Bernardino. They transferred him there from County Emergency. It must be pretty bad. Cissy, please hurry."

"We'll be there as fast as we can."

I hung up the phone and felt Jake's hand squeeze my shoulder. I took a deep breath and repeated what my cousin had told me, then realized she'd said nothing about Uncle Edward's injuries.

"I don't know how bad he's hurt, but she said to hurry." I turned and headed for the bedroom. "Will you call Dotty and Sam? Tell them we're dropping Libby by. I'll get dressed and wake her."

* * *

Uncle Edward looked like a mummy in a hard white body cast. His right arm and leg were suspended from pulleys attached to the ceiling, his head encased in what must have been yards of bandages. I thought instantly of Sam and felt like running away.

Not again! We can't go through this again!

But of course we could. And from the little Aunt Rose knew, this could be far worse than what Sam had suffered.

Jake stood just inside the door to the narrow room, talking quietly with the nurse who had admitted us. We'd been told the doctor, a talented surgeon named Brian Fob, would see us in the morning. It was only four a.m.; we'd have to wait a couple hours for the answers to a million questions.

Aunt Rose leaned forward from a straight-backed chair beside Uncle Edward's head. I marveled at the way she spoke to him, words of comfort and encouragement that he didn't seem to hear, all the while stroking his arm as if he could feel it through the plaster.

I moved up beside her and touched her cheek. "Why didn't you call us sooner, Aunt Rose? We could have waited with you at Emergency."

She smiled. Her eyes looked tired but still full of hope. "I didn't want to worry you, dear. For a while, we didn't know ... And then there was so much to do, with the police report and all. And that poor young man. I wanted to see him, but they wouldn't let me. I wonder if he lived."

Jake put his arms around both of us. "If you mean the boy on the motorcycle, he's still alive."

Mary Margaret glared from the other side of the bed. "He doesn't deserve to be!"

"M," I cautioned, "not so loud." I looked around, relieved that the nurse had left the room. Jake said nothing.

Aunt Rose lifted her head and stared out the window, a sad, sweet smile on her face. "Don't be too hard on him, sweetheart. He didn't set out to hurt your father, you know."

"But the police said the accident was that punk's fault. They said the kid was zipping in and out of traffic like he owned the road. If he'd been obeying the rules, he wouldn't have pulled in front of Daddy and run him off the road." She was trying to talk softly, but her voice rose in pitch until she sounded for all the world like Katharina in *Taming of the Shrew.*

Aunt Rose just sighed and bent her head back to Uncle Edward's ear.

Careful, dear cousin, I thought. *I wouldn't throw too many stones.* Jake drew me out of the room before I could say it aloud.

He pushed the button for the elevator. The numbered lights above the elevator doors flashed green as the car passed each floor, and he stared at them like they were a Christmas light display.

The third-floor light began to blink. A soft bong sounded, and the elevator doors slid open. Once we were inside, an older man dressed in surgical greens smiled wearily and asked, "What floor?"

"Lobby," Jake replied, and we stood silent through the slow descent until the doors slid open once again and deposited the doctor on the second floor.

"I guess the kid's pretty banged up," Jake said when we were alone. "They still don't know for sure if he's going to make it, but they transferred him anyway."

"So he's here now too?"

Jake nodded. "Second floor. Intensive care." I felt my face flush and realized I'd been holding back my own feelings of anger toward the young man on the motorcycle. After all, he was the one responsible.

The elevator lurched downward. "Don't tell Mary Margaret." I brushed a strand of hair from my eyes and realized how bedraggled I must look. "Or Aunt Rose either. At least not until we know for sure."

Jake understood. He guided me off the elevator, turned right and led me down a narrow hall. The green tile floor had a bold yellow stripe painted down the middle. It made me dizzy, and I was grateful for my husband's steady hand beneath my elbow.

"Here." He handed me a dime and pointed to a pay phone on the wall behind an empty food-service cart. "Call Dotty and see how Libby's doing while I order us some breakfast." I nodded and watched him disappear through the double doors to the cafeteria.

There was a time, after Pearl Harbor, when we had wondered if Jake was going to make it—a time of waiting when we didn't know if he had lived or died. For a moment those old fears and feelings overwhelmed me.

I closed my eyes and whispered, *Thank God he's alive.* In my heart of hearts I knew I meant them all: Jake, Sam and Uncle Edward. Even the boy on the motorcycle.

Chapter
Eight

"Mama, is Grandpa Ed going to die?"

"No, Libby. Grandpa Ed will be just fine. Why, the doctor said he can even go home in a week or so. Then you can visit him. Won't that be nice?"

Thank God I could tell her that.

It had been six weeks since the accident, and the first three had been touch and go. While they were pretty sure he would live, no one seemed to know if he would walk or talk again. Then, on the third Sunday after the accident, he opened his eyes and asked for a cup of coffee.

"I couldn't believe my ears," Aunt Rose told me later that afternoon. "After three weeks of being unconscious, he wakes up and asks for coffee, of all things! He said it twice, and I could see the twinkle in his eyes. Then he went back to sleep. I laughed till I cried."

Uncle Edward's sleep from then on had been natural and easy. The doctors said he would recover his speech, and his hearing seemed okay. What we didn't know yet was which parts would work and which wouldn't. Besides the fractured skull and broken limbs, he had cuts, abrasions, and several cracked ribs. It would be months before we had all the answers.

Libby loved her "Grandpa Ed," as she called her great-uncle, almost as much as she loved her father. But this was the first time she'd asked if he might die.

I told Jake about it later that evening. "I'm glad she waited until now to ask."

"What do you think brought it on?"

"I'm not sure. There's Anne's Frank, of course, but that was two years ago. It might have been the Plunge."

Jake raised his eyebrows.

"Dotty and Sam's pool pump is on the fritz, so we took the kids to the park to swim, but the Plunge was all locked up. The sign said CLOSED DUE TO POLIO EPIDEMIC. Of course, then we had to explain polio to all of them.

"Libby and Rachel were the only ones who understood a thing we said. Well, maybe David, but he was so busy teasing the twins I don't think he heard a word. Anyway, Rachel asked if people died from polio, and what could we say? We had to tell her yes. Thank God, J. Joe got tired of David's teasing and bit him on the arm. David howled like a banshee and woke the baby, so we had enough distraction to make it home without any more hard questions."

Jake rolled his eyes and hid behind his newspaper. I snatched it from his hands, rolled it into a tube and swatted him on the arm. "That was when Libby asked about Uncle Edward—after we dropped off Dotty and the kids and came home."

"When is Dotty going to learn to drive?" Jake ducked what would have been a great shot to the head.

"Jake Freeman, quit changing the subject!" I tossed the paper out of reach and plopped down on his lap. "Libby's eleven. Her questions will only get harder. We'll have to be prepared to deal with them when they come."

Jake frowned. "Like what?"

"Oh, things like death and boys and being a woman."

"That's your territory. I draw the line at teaching her how to wear nail polish and lipstick."

I brushed a lock of thick brown hair off his forehead. He usually slicked it back with VO5, but after his evening shower he just rubbed it dry with a towel and let it be. "What about . . . you know . . . boy/girl things." I felt my face go red, but I knew the time was coming. Rachel had already asked Dot how Mrs. Jones's baby got into her stomach.

Jake looked shocked. "You mean sex? Celia, the child is eleven years old. She won't need to know any of that for years."

I smiled at the look on his face and rubbed the evening shadow on his cheek. "Not that long, darling. Times have changed. Children grow up faster now."

Jake sighed and pulled me closer, nuzzling my neck. "Like you said, babe, we'll deal with that when it comes."

* * *

Dotty was a gem. I would never have survived the weeks after Uncle Edward's accident without her. She watched Libby so I could go back and forth to San Bernardino. It was a two-hour drive from our home in San Gabriel, and I went as often as I could to spell Aunt Rose.

Mary Margaret didn't drive. She still worked nights at the Douglas Aircraft factory and was too busy to visit her parents except on weekends. We took her with us at first, but once she learned her father was on the mend, she went less and less.

I understood, or thought I did. She wasn't trying to be selfish or insensitive. She just could not deal with unpleasant circumstances. Uncle Edward's pain and the hospital atmosphere drove her to distraction. She promised to take her vacation time and help out once he came home to recuperate. Jake wasn't convinced that would ever happen.

"She's too shallow, Celia. She'll find some excuse, you wait and see."

"I hope he's wrong," I told Dotty one Saturday as we un-loaded groceries from the car. Jake and Sam were at her house watching a ball game and keeping an eye on the kids so we could shop in peace. "They've done a lot for that girl since the divorce. You'd think she'd want to give something back."

"She'll come around."

"I hope so." I went around to the driver's side and slid behind the wheel. I'd been driving for three years now, since Libby was in third grade and we'd realized how much she needed to be carted around. Jake had saved money from his overtime pay at the garage and bought me a 1950 Chevy. Now I couldn't imag-ine being without it.

Dotty climbed into the passenger's seat.

"When are you going to learn to drive?"

She looked wounded. "Why? Are you getting tired of hauling me around?"

"Of course not! It's just that I don't see how you manage with five kids and no transportation most of the time."

She shrugged. "It's not that bad. We run most of our errands after Sam gets home from work. Anyway, we don't go very far. With my brood it's easier to stay home."

"No, really, Dot, why don't you get Sam to teach you? It's fun."

"Someday."

I could tell she was getting uncomfortable, so I dropped the subject. But only a week later, fear for her children caused her to take her first lesson.

She had been out back hanging the wash. Rachel and David were in school, but the twins were just getting over measles and had a day or two left at home. They got everything in tandem: chicken pox, mumps, even poison ivy. We never did find out where they came up with that.

Zeke was taking his afternoon nap and the twins were in the living room watching Sheriff John cartoons. Sarah told her mother later how she'd looked out the window and saw her cat Muffin sunning herself on the lawn while the Sampsons' German shepherd, Butch, was sniffing his way up the street. She put two and two together and raced out the door to the rescue.

According to J. Joe, she scooped up the cat just as Butch hit the sidewalk in front of the house. Muffin caught sight of the dog, and the dog caught sight of Muffin.

The next day, a sober Sarah, swathed in bandages and lapping up a bowl of ice cream, explained it all to me. "I screamed at Butch to get away, but he kept jumping up at Muffy and she scratched me."

Dotty shuddered and brushed a piece of lint off her daughter's shaved head. "It was awful, Celia. I heard her screams from clear out back. By the time I got out there the cat was halfway up the elm tree and J. Joe was chasing Butch down the street with a baseball bat."

"I was blooding," Sarah declared solemnly and licked her spoon.

"That's an understatement," Dotty continued. "The doctor said the cat must have run right up over her face and head. It's a miracle she didn't scratch an eye out.

"I screamed for help, but nobody came, so I carried her inside and washed the cuts as best I could. Thank God, Sam pulled in the drive just minutes later, and we rushed her to Dr. Farmer's office.

"It was right after that when Sam laid down the law. 'That settles it, Dot,' he said. 'I'm getting you a car for emergencies. I want you to call a driving school and start lessons tomorrow.'

"He sounded like a drill sergeant, Celia," Dotty sighed. "But he's right. I can't put it off any longer. I have to learn to drive."

Chapter
Nine

In the woods that surround Bear Lake, there are stands of oak
and cedar among the pine, and mile-wide open meadows with
grass so tall a full-grown elk can stand up and not be seen.

A few hundred yards above the lake, on the west side where
only wild things enjoy the sun, water gushes from the smooth
gray rock and feeds a pool as round and blue as one of Mama's
old china plates.

Jake and I camped there the summer before Mama died. We
set up his father's old canvas army tent in a clearing just above
the pond, and spent a week exploring. We fished, followed deer
trails, and soaked up peace and quiet like sunshine on a rock.

By the time we left, Jake had tamed a half-grown raccoon
into taking fish scraps from his fingers. We wanted to take it
home with us, both the coon and the quiet, but, like the Bible
says, there's a time and season for everything. Jake had a job
to go back to, the garden was ready for harvest, and I had to
take Liberty Jane shopping for school. Besides, after a week in
San Bernardino, she had most likely worn out her welcome.
And Aunt Rose's patience.

The avocado grove behind our house was no substitute for
the forest, but it served to calm my mind on those days when

I could slip away through the gate behind the clothesline. It wasn't often I could manage it. Our house was small, but lately it had been a struggle to keep ahead of the laundry, ironing and sewing. "I put it off until the last minute," I told Dotty, "then feel resentful when I have to do it all at once."

"You're just distracted because of your uncle," Dotty assured me. "Things will settle down soon, and you'll get back into a normal routine."

* * *

In late September, Libby came down with the measles on the very day we were supposed to bring Uncle Edward home from the hospital. I had to call Mary Margaret and tell her I couldn't go.

"Honestly, Celia! What am I supposed to do, take a bus all the way to San Bernardino?"

I sighed. Leave it to Mary Margaret to make things harder than they had to be. "Not all the way, M, just to the hospital. It's only an hour. You can help your mother get him into the car and she'll drive from there.

"You really should get your license," I added. "It would make things a lot simpler." I couldn't help it if I sounded miffed. Mary Margaret's selfish attitude got to me. To top it off, Libby was wailing into her pillow because she had to miss the first skating party of the school year, and I was the meanest mother in the whole world for making her stay home.

"I can't afford a car," Mary Margaret huffed. "I don't have a husband to support me."

I ignored her whining. She'd made up her mind to stay bitter over her divorce, and nothing the family did seemed to help. "She's cooking in her own stew," Dotty had said. "Let her simmer. She'll get tired of it someday."

I prayed that day would come soon.

"Jake will come down tonight and pick you up. Although it

would be better if you could stay a few days, until Aunt Rose can manage on her own."

"I can't stay long. You know that, Celia. I have to work, and there's my art group on Thursday morning. Besides, Mother will manage just fine. She always does."

By the time I called Jake and got Libby settled with aspirin and cartoons, I was ready to tear my hair out.

I took a load of wash out to the clothesline. I had just pinned up the last of Jake's work shirts when a speckled hawk flew down and brushed the top of the apple tree with his wing. It knocked him off balance for a second, but he recovered instantly and soared into the orchard.

Had he been injured? I peered over the fence, but there was no sign of the hawk, only a few sparrows searching the tree leaves for bugs. I could hear Libby's laughter from the living room. The *Howdy Doody Show* was on, and I knew she'd be content for at least half an hour, so I yielded to temptation and pushed open the redwood gate.

I had to wade through a patch of weeds to reach the tree line. I envisioned flowers planted there and a narrow gravel path leading into the grove. Foolish thoughts—this was someone else's land.

The leaves were a waxy green with just a hint of brown, crinkle-dry and curling on the ends. My feet kicked up dust no matter how carefully I walked. But it was peaceful here and shaded from the late-morning sun. It was the perfect atmosphere to reflect on the months just past.

I knew we still had a "long row to hoe," as Papa would have said. The doctor had predicted three more months of bed rest and perhaps another surgery before Uncle Edward would be well again. To top it off, he'd lost his job at the cookie factory. "After all these years!" Mary Margaret had said, furious. For once, I agreed with her.

"How could they do that to him?" I had ranted at Jake. "After all he's done for them! Why, he took a cut in pay and stuck it out when times were so bad they almost had to close the plant. And he saw that things ran smoothly, even when half the packaging crew were sick."

"Think about it, Celia. They have a business to run. They can't just shut down until Ed is well. Like Jenkins said, they had to hire someone to replace him. If there's an opening, he can come back when he's well. Just be thankful they had insurance."

Jake was right, of course. Mr. Jenkins, the president of the company, had been very apologetic and had told Aunt Rose to call him if there was anything he could do to help.

Lots of people had said that. But what was there for anyone to do?

I felt restless and out of sorts. Just before the accident I had taken to writing letters to adoption agencies, hoping for a lead—some scrap of information that might help in my search for Chuck and Grace. But the results had been disappointing, and I had no idea which way to turn next.

My attempts to find Sister Anne had petered out a long time ago. Once I thought I'd found her working with a Catholic charity group in San Francisco, but it turned out to be another Sister Anne, who'd received her training in New York City and insisted she had never even been to Pasadena.

Jake thought I was crazy. "You're only causing yourself more grief, Celia. Why don't you let it be?"

He didn't say I was causing him grief too, but I knew that was what he meant. From then on I vowed to keep my efforts— and my letters—to myself.

I plucked a green-and-white striped caterpillar from an avocado leaf and watched it inch its way along my arm. If I turned my hand, it would stop a moment, then calmly move ahead, always upward toward the light. Why couldn't I take things in stride like that? Instead I felt like a moth trapped in the porch light, flitting here and there, trying to fight its way out but just knocking itself senseless in the process. Some of them die like that.

Jake had been discontented lately too. He was a great mechanic and made good wages. We had our home and two cars and went out to dinner almost once a week. But he wanted more. It didn't have to do with things. Lord knows we were thankful for the many blessings he had given us. But Jake was bored. "I've advanced as far as I can at the shop, Celia," he'd said just last week. "If I have to work as a mechanic, I might as well open my own place."

He'd said things like that before. When he admitted he'd probably never realize his dream to fly an airplane, he'd talked about a business of his own. But nothing had ever come of it, and I had to admit I was glad.

Then a week or so after Uncle Edward's accident, the auto shop on the corner of Valley and Rosemead went up for sale.

"It's only six blocks from home. I could walk to work and save on gas. How would you like that, babe?"

I didn't say anything, but the plan made me nervous. What would we live on if it didn't work? We had no savings, and with Libby in a private school we couldn't afford to take a cut in pay, let alone lose Jake's steady income altogether.

Jake had been quiet after that, and I thought he had let it go. But last night he'd come home more excited than I'd seen him in months. "We did it, babe!" He grabbed me around the waist and danced with me across the room. "The bank approved our loan, and I've given notice at the shop. By this time next month, your husband will be in business for himself!" He beamed with pride and plopped down breathless on the couch next to Libby, who was staring at us open-mouthed, like we were monkeys in a zoo.

"How about that, sugar? Your dad now owns his own shop."

Her eyes lit up like fireflies on a moonless night. "Does that mean we're rich? Can we get a pool like Aunt Dot and Uncle Sam?"

Jake laughed, but I couldn't bring myself to join the fun.

Dinner was a solemn affair for me, and Libby only picked at her food, but Jake didn't seem to notice. He bubbled on and on about his plans. I listened and tried to stem my anxious thoughts. But with Libby fidgeting and Aunt Rose calling to confirm my help in bringing Uncle Edward home, it was all I could do to be civil.

When I took Libby's temperature, it was 101 degrees, so I gave her aspirin and put her to bed. I did the dishes and mixed the batter for a cake. I heard George Burns on TV and knew I couldn't hide out in the kitchen forever. Jake and I always watched the Burns and Allen show together. I knew I'd have to face him with my fears.

"What about our insurance?" I asked when the show was over. "Look what happened to Uncle Edward. Without insurance they'd be in the poorhouse. He won't be able to work at all for the better part of a year, and we might have to help them out."

Jake scowled. "Don't worry about it, Celia. I'll get insurance. The shop will be a success, you'll see. You won't lack for anything, and neither will Ed and Rose."

I had been too tired to explain my feelings, not that I could have if I'd tried, so I said nothing when he stomped off to the bathroom and slept on his own side of the bed all night. He had left for work as usual at eight o'clock this morning, like there had been no disagreement between us at all. I was the one who was out of sorts, prowling an avocado orchard in the middle of the morning when I should have been doing chores.

Libby's hollering brought me out of my reverie. I looked at my watch. Noon. Where did the time go? I raced back to the yard.

She was standing by the gate, shivering in her bare feet and nightgown. "There you are," she sniffled. "My throat hurts and I itch. Will you fix me chicken soup for lunch? The canned kind, with milk instead of water."

As I put my arm around my daughter's shoulders and led her into the house, I realized I had never found the hawk.

Chapter
Ten

That night Jake came home a little after nine. He looked pale and his shoulders drooped, a sure sign that he was exhausted and probably in pain as well. The wounds he'd received at Pearl Harbor had healed, but the pain had never gone away completely, and the doctors said it probably never would.

He kissed my brow and went straight to our room to change out of his overalls and sweat-stained shirt. When he came into the kitchen, he was rubbing his shoulder and swinging his arm like a windmill. "I'm starved, Celia. Is there anything to eat?"

It always amazed me how he could ask that question when food was bubbling on the stove. But it happened all the time. Did he think I was cooking for someone else?

"I made a pot of vegetable soup, and there's grilled cheese. Do you want one sandwich or two?"

He pulled out a chair and turned it around, straddling the seat and resting his arms on the back. "Better make it two. I've just spent three hours with your cousin. It's either eat or punch a hole in the wall. I think eating is the safer option."

His expression was part grimace, part grin. I set the steaming soup and a glass of milk in front of him, and the grin won out, but only for a moment. I could tell he had a lot on his mind, but I'd learned a long time ago not to push Jake. Prying just made him shut up tighter than a clam on a sunny beach.

"How's Libby?" He drained the milk and held out his glass for more.

I set the bottle on the table, cut the sandwiches diagonally and put them on his plate. He ate the first one in four bites and was halfway through the other before I finished telling him about our day.

"Is Uncle Edward all right?" I asked when he pushed the plate away.

"He's okay. Tired. Rose said the trip home was hard on him, and Mary Margaret wasn't much help."

"Aunt Rose said that?" I was shocked. Aunt Rose never criticized Mary Margaret. I knew she was disappointed in her choices and attitude, but she would never say a thing to anyone else in the family, and wouldn't allow it said in front of her either.

"No, I said that. She started sniveling every time she walked into her father's room. How could she be any help?"

He folded his napkin and tossed it back onto the table. "I tried to talk to her on the way home, but she was too busy wailing about how tired she was. Let's see: her back hurt, her feet hurt, her boss is a jerk—"

"She never said that!"

He nodded. "Worse. Anyway, when she got done with her boss, she started in on Wesley. I tried to bring the subject back to Ed, but that only made matters worse. She spent a full twenty minutes blasting the boy who caused the accident and motorcycles in general. Then she ranted about how unfair her father's injuries were.

"I told her no one ever promised her 'fair,' and that shut her up for the next ten minutes. By then we were at her apartment." He sighed. "She'll probably never speak to me again. Thank God."

Chapter Ten

I couldn't help but laugh. "You poor dear." I stood behind him and rubbed the back of his neck, working my fingers into his shoulder muscles. He groaned, but didn't move away. I knew the massage was working when the muscles began to relax and he sighed in relief.

"I'll call Aunt Rose in the morning," I said. "If Libby's better, maybe we can go down."

"Don't bother. Two of the women from her church are scheduled to come. They'll clean and make up meals. Enough for a week, I think she said."

I worked my way down his back, skimming over the puckered scars beneath his clean T-shirt. The burns had been deep enough to kill the nerves beneath the skin and the area around them was numb.

He was quiet for so long I thought he'd drifted off, like a sleepy child who wouldn't lay his head down. Chuckie used to do that. Mama said he was afraid he'd miss something if he went to sleep. Krista used to pinch herself to stay awake—her upper arms were often black and blue—but Chuckie played. One by one the toys would drop from his tiny hands. His head would nod, and he would start to hum and rock back and forth on his bottom in the middle of the living room floor.

"Lynetta," Papa would say, "put that boy to bed. He's going to fall flat on his face."

Mama just smiled. "He won't hurt himself, Charles. He'll go to sleep faster if he does it on his own."

Sure enough, by the time Mama got the crib railing down and the covers ready, Chuckie would roll slowly to the floor. "Out like a light." Papa would smile and shake his head, then lift him to one shoulder and help Mama tuck him in.

"Celia?" Jake's voice was almost a whisper, but it startled me, and I realized my hands had stopped. I started rubbing again. "Don't," he said. "Come sit." He pushed the other chair out with his foot.

"I had an hour at lunch today and went out to the shop. It'll take some cleaning, and one or two new pieces of equipment, but it's going to work out great. Would you like to see it? You could come with me tomorrow. At noon, if Libby's better."

He wouldn't look me in the eye, and I knew this was a test. The question was: Would I be a loyal wife and back him, or would I let my fears spoil his dream? I whispered a prayer for wisdom.

"Of course I want to see it, Jake. If Libby's well enough we'll meet you there tomorrow."

Later, when I thought we were both half asleep, Jake suddenly rolled onto his back. "Oh, I forgot. Rose said to tell you the boy is out of danger. It will take a while, but the doctors think he'll be okay."

Chapter
Eleven

Most people thought Aunt Rose was crazy for being so concerned about the boy. But I understood. "What if it were Billy lying there?" she had said a few days after the accident. "We'd surely want someone to care enough to visit him, even if he doesn't know they're there. His poor parents must be frantic with worry."

"She's right about that," I told Jake as we left the hospital a few weeks later after a visit to Uncle Edward. "Surely there's someone looking for him. I can't believe they still don't know his name or where he comes from."

Jake opened the car door for me and went around to the other side. We were halfway out of the parking lot before he answered.

"I can believe it. You didn't see him, Celia. They let me go in with Rose today."

"You went in to see him? Where was I?"

"You and Mary Margaret were at the gift shop. Ed was sound asleep, and Rose insisted that we visit 'John.' That's what the nurses call him. Makes it easier to remember there's a person under all those bandages."

I hadn't had the nerve to go when Aunt Rose asked me the

week before. I'd made up an excuse about someone needing to stay with Uncle Edward. The truth of it was, hospitals made me queasy. It was hard enough to see Uncle Edward in this condition. How could I bear to visit a stranger, especially when I knew he was pretty messed up? I pushed away the guilt and turned my attention back to Jake.

"He wasn't carrying any ID. Not even a driver's license, which means he's in trouble. If he lives, that is."

I frowned. "Can't they trace the bike or match him to a missing person report or something?"

"The bike was registered to a thirty-year-old artist in Laguna Beach. Turns out it was stolen the day before the accident. So our John has even more strikes against him. As for matching him to a missing person report," Jake shrugged, "the only things not bandaged are his nose and toes, so fingerprints are out."

Now, with Uncle Edward home, I thought Aunt Rose would give up her visits to John. But I was wrong.

* * *

Libby's rash had disappeared by Friday, and by Monday morning I was thankful she could go back to school.

"That girl wasn't cut out to be an invalid," I told Aunt Rose when I telephoned to check on her and Uncle Edward. "She nearly drove me to distraction. I don't know what was worse— when she was sick and whined, or when she felt better and kept saying how bored she was. Dot and I finally gave in and had Rachel over all day Saturday. You'd have thought they'd been separated for years instead of just six days."

"That's nice, dear." I could tell her mind wasn't on Dotty or Liberty Jane, so I changed the subject.

"Is Uncle Edward up again today?" I knew he was supposed to try to move around a little each day, but by Wednesday he'd insisted on walking out to the garden and back, with Aunt Rose there to steady him. Nonetheless, it proved to be too much, and he'd had to take an extra pill that night for pain. Knowing Uncle Edward, I was sure that didn't stop him from trying again.

"My, yes! Nothing I say can stop that man. He's determined to be out and about, in spite of the pain. We see the doctor on Friday. Maybe he can talk some sense into him.

"Which reminds me, Cissy: you'll be glad to know our John is out of the coma. When I called to make Edward's appointment, Dr. Fob said the boy was alert. He's not talking yet and seems confused when they ask him too many questions. I guess the police are going to try for information again tomorrow."

The phone line went quiet, but I knew there was more she wanted to say.

"I think one of us should be there, Cissy. I keep thinking how Billy would feel, confused and in pain, being questioned by the police. John shouldn't be alone."

Did she expect me to say I would go? My heart pounded at the thought. He didn't know me, hadn't even heard my voice. How could I comfort him?

"I know you have your hands full, dear, with Libby and all, but do you think you could come? You could sit with Uncle Edward in the doctor's office while I run up to see John." Aunt Rose's voice had taken on a pleading sound I'd never heard from her before, and I realized this meant a lot to her.

"I'll go, of course," I told Dotty later that afternoon. "But I'm worried about her. Do you think she's getting too involved? I mean, he did steal that motorcycle. And no ID. What if it turns out the boy's a murderer or something? Aunt Rose could even be in danger."

Dotty wasn't impressed. "Don't stew so, girl. Your aunt is the most level-headed woman I know. She's not going to get into trouble. When God passed out attributes, he gave Aunt Rose an extra helping of compassion. I'd say the boy needs someone exactly like her right now."

I knew she was right. At least about him needing Aunt Rose. Still, I knew from experience that evil touches even the innocent, and Aunt Rose's giving nature wouldn't necessarily protect her from harm.

Maybe not, but God can. Still, what if he chooses not to? The debate with myself went on the rest of the afternoon. By the time Libby dragged in from school, I felt as bedraggled as she looked.

"You're so pale, darling." I laid my hand against her forehead. It felt cool, but that didn't necessarily mean anything. "I knew we let you go back too soon."

"Oh, Mother, I'm all right. But Mrs. Roberts wouldn't let me stay in from recess without a note. She said she tried to call you, but the line was busy. I had to help turn the jumprope for a bunch of little kids." She rolled her eyes, then flung her books and sweater on the kitchen table. "Please, please, give me a note tomorrow." She hung her head and then looked up through soft brown lashes. It was a practiced look that didn't fool me for a minute. "If I stay inside I can catch up on all my reading."

I laughed. Libby had disliked recess from the second day of school when she learned that Rachel's fifth-grade class had a different playground slot than her sixth-grade one. She had other friends, but she insisted they'd gotten too stuck-up over the summer and didn't want to play with her anymore. I suspected they just needed to get reacquainted, and I secretly had been pleased that she would be forced to play with someone besides Rachel. Not that I didn't love Rachel to death. All of Dotty's brood were as dear to me as my own. But Dot and I agreed the girls needed to make other friends as well. This was the perfect opportunity.

I patted Libby's cheek and realized she was nearly holding

her breath waiting for an answer. "I'll write a note to Mrs. Roberts right now."

Her eyes lit up like the sun peeking from behind a cloud.

"But only for one more day. You should be fine by Wednesday, and the fresh air is good for you."

She pouted, but only for a moment. Libby was never one to sulk.

*　*　*

On Tuesday morning I felt restless and out of sorts. With Libby in school all day and Jake working longer hours at the shop, I needed something besides laundry and dishes to turn my mind to.

All my efforts to find Chuck and Grace had come to nothing, and for a time I'd given it up as lost. But like Grandma Eva always said, "You'll never have soup if you don't stir the pot." So I decided to make one last effort.

"The only thing I haven't really tried," I told Dotty, "is to find Sister Anne after running into that one dead end." I knew that even if I did find her, it was unlikely she'd be willing to tell me more than the others. But there was always a chance. After all, she'd been nice to me, and she had a soft spot for Chuck.

Dotty was skeptical but agreed it was worth a try. "You surely won't be content," she said, "until you've upturned every stone."

I dropped Libby at school the next morning and, instead of going straight home to start the wash, turned left on San Gabriel Boulevard and headed up to Pasadena.

Just as I had hoped, the Huntington Library had the books and directories I needed. It took almost four hours to copy down the addresses. But by the time I was through, I knew I could contact every convent and Catholic organization in the state of California.

I spent a good chunk of my household money on envelopes

and stamps. Jake didn't notice that we had hamburger three times that week instead of twice, but he did ask why I wasn't eating it.

"I must have a touch of something," I told him. That was no lie. Suddenly everything tasted like glue, and my stomach rebelled at the sight of food.

Chapter
Twelve

On the day of Uncle Edward's appointment, Mary Margaret showed up on my doorstep at eight o'clock in the morning. She clutched her suitcase in one hand and her pillow in the other. "I'm worried about Mother," she announced. "She doesn't seem herself, so I took four days' vacation to go and help."

She expected me to drive her. I felt a jab of irritation but reminded myself I'd planned on going out there anyway.

If Aunt Rose was surprised to see her, she didn't show it. She kissed us both and pointed toward the bedroom. "Edward's been ready to go for an hour." She sounded exasperated. "That man! I can't do a thing with him. He'll talk the doctor into taking the casts off early, you just wait and see."

When we got to the hospital, Uncle Edward waved Aunt Rose toward the elevators and balanced awkwardly on the edge of the waiting-room sofa. "Go see the boy, Rose. I'm anxious to know what they found out."

She'd been gone half an hour before the nurse called Uncle Edward in. "You girls stay here," he said, allowing the nurse to help him to his feet. "If Rose gets back, tell her I'll manage fine. She doesn't need to come in."

Ten minutes later, Aunt Rose came back so excited I thought

she would wear out the carpet between the waiting room and the nurses' station.

"John smiled at me, Cissy, and squeezed my hand. I think he recognized my voice!"

Mary Margaret looked up from her *Ladies Home Journal.* "Honestly, Mother, you're more concerned about that juvenile delinquent than you are about Daddy."

I poked her arm, but she just glared me down and went back to the article she was reading.

I knew Mary Margaret's comment wasn't true. Aunt Rose looked first and foremost after Uncle Edward's welfare. But both of them really cared about the young man and his struggle. I wondered if I could be so forgiving if it had been Jake he'd almost killed.

"He's in a lot of pain," Aunt Rose said, ignoring Mary Margaret and sitting down on the arm of my chair. "Physical and emotional too, I would guess. He still won't talk, although he seems to understand what's said to him. I told him I'd come back tomorrow; that's when he squeezed my hand." Her smile brightened, and she looked at Mary Margaret. "Now that you're here, dear, I can keep my promise."

Aunt Rose had been right about the casts. Uncle Edward shuffled out of the treatment room supported by two young aids in candy-stripe uniforms. He looked pale, his skin white and shriveled where the headgear and plaster had been.

Dr. Fob appeared in the doorway and beckoned Aunt Rose. "I'm not sure about this, Mrs. Crandall," he said, nodding in Uncle Edward's direction, "but your husband's very persuasive. We'll start physical therapy tomorrow. If the pain is too severe, or if anything looks inflamed or swollen, call me right away."

He sighed. "Try to get him to rest. If he does too much too soon, he could end up back in here."

The last sentence was loud enough for the entire hospital to hear, but Uncle Edward pretended not to. "Come on, girls," he called to Mary Margaret and me. "As much as I hate to give up these two beautiful ladies, you'd better take their places and help me to the car."

"Oh no you don't, Mr. Crandall. Here's Susan with the wheelchair." One of the nurses, a pretty blonde in a starched white uniform, eased him backward until he had no choice but to fall into the waiting chair.

* * *

While Aunt Rose and Mary Margaret made tuna sandwiches in the kitchen, I helped Uncle Edward into a red metal patio chair and rolled up a beach towel to fit behind his neck.

"Ah, that does feel good, Celia. Thank you."

I could see the creases of pain etched across his face. The scars gleamed pink and swollen from beneath a Brillo-pad patch of hair just starting to grow back. I reached to touch them, then drew my hand away. Chuckie had a scar like that on his cheek, just beneath his eye where Papa had smacked him.

What a set-to that was. Papa had come home drunk and stepped on Tarzan's tail, and Chuckie bit Papa on the leg. Papa's ring caught him right across the face. The cut took several stitches, and Papa cried. I hated Papa then. But only for that night. He'd been so sweet and sorry afterward.

"Celia, I've been thinking." Uncle Edward's chuckle brought me back to the present. "Actually that's all I've been able to do. Anyway, I don't want to get your hopes up, but I got in touch with Detective Harman a week or so ago . . ." He must have noticed my frown. "Now don't get your dander up. I know he's not Mister Personality, but you have to admit he's good at what he does."

If he was so good, why had it taken him so long to catch up with those creeps who tried to kill Sam and me? But I kept my thoughts to myself. That whole mess was over long ago. There was no need to resurrect old ghosts. "He retired a year ago, but he still has connections. He said he'd snoop around and see what he can find out about Chuck and Grace."

I was stunned. I thought everyone but me had given up searching for them years ago.

"He knows some judge—Randall, I think his name is. He thinks the laws should be changed to allow adopted children over the age of twenty-one to see their own records. Now I know that's not the same as releasing them to us, but Harman thinks if we write an appeal and a letter of explanation, Judge Randall might be sympathetic to the case."

I didn't know what to say. I hadn't told anyone but Dotty about my letters, and so far they hadn't produced any results. Maybe Detective Harman could help.

Uncle Edward must have thought I was upset. "It's entirely up to you, sweetheart." With an effort, he lifted his hand and laid it against my cheek. "If it's too painful for you, we'll just drop it."

I took his paste-white hand between my own, kissed it and lowered it back to a comfortable position on his lap. "No," I said. "If there's a way, we have to try."

Chapter
Thirteen

The smell of Sunday-morning bacon usually had Libby out of bed and into the kitchen before the first pancake hit the griddle. When she wasn't in her chair by the time I poured Jake's coffee, I went to investigate.

"Liberty Jane, why are you still in bed? Are you sick?"

"I'm fine, Mom." She flashed a sleepy smile and let me feel her forehead. "See?"

I wasn't convinced. She was always wide awake by seven and eager to get on with her day. Libby was all girl, but as spry and active as a boy. She could be giggling with her friends one minute and running races with the boys the next. She often beat them too. I smiled. She reminded me of myself at that age.

Libby yawned loudly, stretched, then turned over on her side.

"Well then, sleepyhead, you'd better rise and shine. Breakfast is ready, and you'll be late for Sunday school."

"I think I'll just stay home today."

I sat down on the edge of her bed. "All right, young lady," I said, rolling her gently onto her back, "what's this all about? You love Sunday school. Why don't you want to go?"

"What's going on?" Jake appeared in the doorway. "Celia, the bacon is fried to a crisp." His tone held both irritation and concern, like the papa bear who'd just discovered his porridge missing.

"Oh, grief!" I started for the kitchen, but he held up his hand.

"I turned it off." He looked at Libby. "Is she sick?"

I shook my head. "Libby, either tell me what's wrong or get up this minute."

"But Mom," she wailed and sat up, pulling the covers to her chin. "The hayride is tomorrow night after school, and I need my beauty sleep."

Jake rolled his eyes and turned away so fast he spilled coffee all over the hall floor. I could hear him laughing as he headed into the bathroom for a towel.

"Not my good ones!" I hollered after him. "Use the green rag. And stop laughing!"

I had to stifle a chuckle myself, but I knew we had to deal with the source of this before it got out of hand. And I suspected I knew who the source was.

"Liberty Jane, where did you get that nonsense?"

She looked offended. "It's not nonsense, Mother. I asked Aunt M why she doesn't go to church. She said she needed her beauty sleep, and Sunday was the only time she could get it.

"She goes to parties all the time and always looks so pretty. I want to be pretty too, so Peter will sit next to me instead of Ellen."

Leave it to Mary Margaret!

Jake looked up from the hallway where he'd been mopping up coffee and flashed me a look that clearly said, *You handle this, she's your cousin.* Then he headed back to the kitchen. Soon I could hear him plopping batter onto the griddle, and I knew we'd have to get this settled fast or we'd all be late for church.

"Okay, Libby, we'll talk about Peter and Ellen later. As for your 'beauty sleep,' you're beautiful enough as it is." I smoothed her hair and kissed her sleep-warm brow. "Up. Right now, or

I'll give your share of breakfast to your father." I swatted her leg through the covers to let her know I meant business and retreated to the kitchen to rescue Jake.

Not that he couldn't manage in a kitchen. As the oldest in a family of eight children, he'd done his share of household chores and more. But Mama had always been the one to do the cooking and cleaning at our house, like Grandma Eva before her. Besides, there was nothing more satisfying to me than a well-ordered home. A labor of love, Aunt Rose called it, and I agreed.

I heard the water turn on in the bathroom upstairs and took the spatula away from Jake. "Here, sit down, I'll get you another stack. Honestly, I'd like to strangle that Mary Margaret. What a thing to say to an eleven-year-old girl!"

"You'll have to talk to your cousin, Celia. She's only using that beauty-sleep routine as an excuse. She can make her own choices, but I don't want her influencing Libby."

When it came down to it, I knew sleep had nothing to do with it. When Wesley had served her with divorce papers, shortly before the end of the war, Mary Margaret had blamed him for carousing with other women, and she had blamed God for allowing it to happen. Never mind that everyone had tried to warn her about him. She had insisted on marrying him. No one in the family said anything afterward. There was never a hint of reproof or "I told you so" from any of us. For months we'd treated her like a hothouse flower, calling every day, inviting her to dinner and a show now and then. Even Sam and Dotty had gone out of their way to include her in our social life.

"I'm busy," she had replied to every invitation to go with us to church. But after several months she began to give in.

"All right, Celia, I'll come to church with you next Sunday. Lord knows you won't leave me alone until I do! What should I wear?"

"First Baptist is just like the church you grew up in," I told her. "Just wear a nice dress."

After four or five visits, her demeanor softened. "It's amazing how well I remember all the old hymns," she said. "Donna Struthers thinks I should join the choir. I told her I'd think about it and let her know."

We always stood around after a service to greet each other and catch up on the latest news. To my surprise, Mary Margaret took full advantage of that time. "Look at her," I whispered to Dotty and pointed to a small group of women gathered by the foot of the balcony stairs. "She's actually made new friends."

Then she had the misfortune to draw the attention of Mrs. Edna Livermore and her sister, Eunice.

Edna Livermore's husband had been killed at Normandy. Shortly after, she came to live with her sister and share the burden of their aging, invalid father. The sister, Eunice Wagington, had never married and delighted in delving into other people's private lives. It wasn't long before she had Edna thoroughly engrossed in the sport, and First Baptist Church was their happy hunting ground.

One Sunday, after a particularly moving sermon about Jesus and the woman at the well, I saw Mary Margaret standing in a corner of the foyer with a younger single girl. The sisters Livermore and Wagington had perched on chairs only a few feet away, all but falling over each other trying to hear the conversation.

I tried to catch Mary Margaret's eye, but she was too engrossed in her story to see my frantic waving, so I eased through the crowd and came up behind them. Too late, I realized she was entertaining the girl with the gory details of her divorce. And the good sisters were following every word like hounds on the scent. Sure enough, by the next Sunday the somewhat embellished details of Mary Margaret's "shameful secret" were common knowledge among the congregation.

To be fair, most people ignored the gossip and greeted Mary Margaret as usual. But some chose to believe the uglier aspects of the story and avoided her like the plague. By the time a few loyal friends had reported what they had heard to Mary Margaret, she'd been treed, trussed and thrown to the dogs.

"I'd like to tie their tongues in a knot!" I cried to Jake. "Things like that should not happen at church."

Jake talked to Pastor Willis, who took the astonished sisters to task, then called Mary Margaret to apologize. But the damage was done.

"If those nasty old biddies are an example of Christian charity, I want no part of it," she said. And that was the end of it. Nothing we said could sway her. "I'll never darken the door of a church again," she insisted.

"Wouldn't you know," I told Dotty later, "that would be the one promise Mary Margaret would keep."

Chapter
Fourteen

A few days later I heard from Sister Anne. Out of almost fifty letters, I received only four replies. Three had come just days after my inquiries had been sent. They were all short and to the point: "There is no one from St. Stephen's here." The fourth envelope wasn't much fatter than the others: two pages of notepaper adorned with loosely scrawled cursive. My heart did flips when I saw who it was from.

My dear Mrs. Freeman,

Your letter reached me at Greenwood Abbey a few days ago. I must say I knew right away who you were and what your mission was, but I confess I've been reluctant to answer.

I'm sure you've suffered no end of heartache over the loss of your brother and sister, and I will regret forever my part in deceiving you, but the Reverend Mother thought it best to get the little ones off without a fuss.

As to where they went, and with whom, I know the couple who picked them up that day were well-to-do. It seems to me the Reverend Mother called him "Doctor," and San Diego was mentioned. Beyond that, I have nothing to offer.

I wish I could give you more information. The children will

be grown by now, and I see no harm in a reunion. Please let me know if your search proves fruitful. God grant you hope and peace.

It was signed "Anne Finnigan."

I felt suddenly lightheaded and plopped myself into Jake's reclining chair. Her letter was not very promising, but it had given me two clues. How hard would it be to find a doctor with adopted children in a city the size of San Diego?

"Impossible," was Jake's verdict. But I knew I had to try.

* * *

When the phone rang Monday morning at half past nine, Chaplain Drain was the last person I would have expected. I had quit working for him and Captain Long shortly before Libby was born, and we'd lost touch with them both a year or so later. "Celia, how are you? I saw Jake at the brake shop the other day. He looks good, and he assured me his wounds have healed completely. Says your Libby is really growing up."

I felt a flash of guilt. The chaplain had been the most important link in the chain of events that led to Jake's emotional recovery after Pearl Harbor. And he had helped me countless times as well. How could we have let him drift out of our lives?

True to his military background, he got right down to business. "I retired a year ago, and my daughter has decided I'd be less of a worry to them if I were in their own back yard, so to speak." I could hear the smile in his quiet voice. "I'm moving back to Michigan and have to give up my position on the board of the Children's Charities Association."

He cleared his throat. "At our last meeting the president mentioned an urgent need for part-time secretarial help. Volunteer, of course. When I ran into Jake, you came to mind."

While I scrambled to form some sort of reply, he hurried on. "Children's Charities organizes fund-raisers for underprivileged children. We help the social service agencies monitor foster homes and assist with the paperwork when a child is placed for adoption.

"It's a worthy organization, Celia. With your typing and organizational skills, you'd be a real asset to the group. Will you think about it? Take your time, and let me know next week."

He mentioned some more details about the job, then I jotted down his number and managed a good-by. Volunteer, he had said. Well, paid or not, it was a job—and the last thing I needed was another job. Yet the prospect made me tingle with excitement. I could brush up on my typing skills, meet new people and help children in the process. Then my mind latched onto a thought and wouldn't let it go.

We assist with paperwork when a child is placed for adoption.

As a secretary, I'd have access to records. I could learn the procedures, look at some files and maybe, just maybe, unravel more threads that would lead me to Chuck and Grace.

My mind was made up. Now all I had to do was convince Jake.

It wasn't easy.

"I don't like the thought of you traipsing around L.A., Celia," Jake said that night after dinner. "The city's not a good place for a woman alone. Don't you have enough to do around here?" He frowned. "And if you're downtown typing and filing, who'll pick up Libby from school?"

I resented his tone and the implication that I couldn't take care of myself in L.A. I'd worked before, and in a worse neighborhood than where the CCA offices were located.

"It won't interfere with you or Libby," I promised. "It's only ten hours a week, and I can set my own schedule. Besides," I pointed out, "you know how fast I type. I'll have the work done in eight."

In the end I won, but it wasn't a pleasant victory. Jake made it clear that I was going against his wishes, and Libby, bless her heart, decided that I should be room mother for the last half of the school year.

"But Mom," she whined when I told her it just wasn't possible, "they're counting on you. You always take a turn."

"Not this year, Libby. You know I just took that job. I'll help out with the party in June, I promise."

She stiffened, preparing for battle, but I patted her cheek and turned back to my closet. "Come help me decide what to wear the first day."

"Mother! You have to. I already told them ... Ouch! Why are you pulling my hair?"

"I'm not pulling, I'm uncovering your ears so you can hear me." I smoothed her tangled curls back over her temples. "I'm sorry, Libby, but you'll just have to untell them. Don't worry, honey. January is over two months away; they'll find someone else."

I fished my old crepe blouse and navy skirt from the rack behind my summer dresses and wondered if I could still wear something that had fit me in 1946.

"You might as well not wear anything." Libby's tone could have frozen fire. "All your clothes are so frumpy!"

Lord help us, I thought as my daughter glared at me and stalked out of the room, *she sounds just like Mary Margaret.*

* * *

My first day on the job went better than I'd imagined. Commander Drain drove me into town, "just so you'll know the way." He confessed, "Actually, it would be better for you to take the bus, it's safer; traffic is terrible down here."

I had to agree. But I liked the job and the people right away. They seemed pleased that I could start so soon, and I was a little disappointed when I finished that day's correspondence in just under three hours.

"Don't worry," the board president, Mr. Johnson, said, laying a friendly hand on my shoulder. "There'll be much more to do next week. Now that you're here, none of us will have to work overtime."

"I like it," I told Jake that evening. "It feels good to get back to work again."

"Only a few hours a week," he cautioned. But he reached into his wallet and drew out a five-dollar bill. "Here, you'll need to make some new clothes."

I thought I heard a note of pride in his voice.

* * *

Aunt Rose called the next morning.

"I think you should come out, Cissy." She sounded like she'd run all the way to the garden and back. "I know it's a long drive and you were just here, but this is important." She paused and took a deep breath. "Jake should come too, if he can."

"Aunt Rose . . . ?"

"I'm sorry, dear. I know I'm being vague. Oh, Cissy please, just come. It's good news, but I don't want to share it over the phone."

Jake couldn't go, of course. "I'm sorry, Celia," he said when I asked him. "You know I would if I could get away, but I promised the Hendershots they'd have their car by noon. They're good customers. If I play my cards right, they'll follow me to Freeman's Repair and Service when we open."

He caught the corner of my mouth with his. "I'll run Libby to school for you. Call me when Rosebud decides to tell you the news." He snickered. "I'll bet our John is up and running races. They've probably adopted him and brought him home."

I had to admit I'd been thinking the same thing. "Our John" had been uppermost in Aunt Rose and Uncle Edward's minds for months. Ever since we knew Uncle Edward would recover, the boy had been their main concern.

"He's so alone, lying there—maybe dying—without anyone

to claim him. Someone has to care."

I felt guilty and ashamed when they said that. They never once chided me for not wanting to visit him. They just accepted my excuses: "He's unconscious; he won't even know I'm there." Then, later, "He has you, Aunt Rose. He doesn't need another stranger prowling around his room."

When I thought it out, I realized my feelings toward John were too close to Mary Margaret's for comfort. Oh, I didn't hate the boy, but he *was* a juvenile delinquent. He had broken the law and had almost killed Uncle Edward.

I can forgive him, I thought as I slipped into my new black flats and gathered up my sweater and purse. *That doesn't mean I have to hold his hand.*

I was halfway to San Bernardino before it hit me. What if the good news wasn't about John at all? What if Uncle Edward had found Chuck and Grace? My heart suddenly hammered in my chest, and I tried not to think about it. If I did, I'd be crazy before I got there. I switched on the radio.

"Remember, Lucky Strike means fine tobacco."

"Call for Philip Morris."

"I'd walk a mile for a Camel."

On the fourth station a young man was singing something about rocks and clocks. The music was loud enough to give me a headache, and the lyrics didn't make any sense. I gave up and twisted the radio knob to off.

By the time I pulled into the driveway I was a bundle of nerves.

Aunt Rose didn't even hug me. She just grabbed my hand and pulled me into the living room. I fully expected to see my brother sitting on the sofa, or some young woman with a familiar face. But there was no one else in the room.

Uncle Edward sat on a dining-room chair, one leg stretched in front of him like it was still in its cast. He balanced his crutches in one hand and clutched a dark-blue binder in the other.

"Sit down, sweetheart." He pointed to his brown recliner a few steps away. "Did you have a good drive?"

Aunt Rose edged toward the kitchen, rubbing her hands into her apron and smiling to beat the band. "I'll get you a cup of tea. Edward?"

"Nothing for me, Rose."

He held up the notebook. "Detective Harman brought this by at seven this morning. He said a friend of his at L.A. Central owed him a favor." Uncle Edward looked uncomfortable. "Normally I wouldn't agree to anything dishonest, but in this case I think we have the right." He handed me the book. "We only have a couple of hours to read it and get it back to him."

My hands shook so, I nearly dropped the narrow binder. Aunt Rose placed a flowered china teacup on the lamp table next to the chair. I took a sip and hoped the camomile with honey would calm my nerves.

I recognized the writing even before I read the first sentence. It was so much like my own—long and curvy, slanted to the left, with bold, wide loops for the little L's and G's, and the dots above the I's floating anywhere above the word.

I ran my hand over the page, caressing it as if it were a puppy or a kitten. Chuck or Grace? Whose hands had turned the pages and held the pen that wrote the words? My eyes blurred. I looked up at Uncle Edward. He nodded and smiled. A reassuring smile. Like Papa's when I had to read aloud or learn the lines for a school play. "You can do it, Pumpkin," he'd say. "Everything will be just fine."

I took a deep breath and looked at the name on the cover. Chuck, then. I turned to the first page and began to read my brother's life.

Chapter
Fifteen

My name is Charles Byron Summers DuVal. Looks good on paper. In reality, it stinks! Like my life.

I can't believe I'm writing this all down. I feel like an idiot girl whining to her diary. This notebook is the only thing I have that's mine. I bought it. After I hocked my guitar, rented this gutter-dump of a room, and bought bread and cheese for dinner, I had a dollar left over so I said what the hey and bought the binder. I chose this one because it came with paper. I couldn't afford to pay extra for paper.

I can't believe that either. Chuck "The Duck" DuVal is broke. Flat-line broke, like a cadaver on my old man's table. Of course he'd say it's my own fault. My choice to ditch it all, make like a bird and fly. And he'd be right. But then, of course, he always is.

The old man's not my real father. I called my real father Papa. But you gotta dig, I was only four and we all called him that. Cissy and me, and even Mama. Krista too, for awhile. I don't remember Krista much. I was pretty little when she died, but I remember Mama cried when the men carried Krista away. They wrapped her in a sheet and took her off. Just like that.

For weeks I crawled out of my crib and slept on the floor,

scared to death they'd come back, wrap me in my sheet and take me away too. I guess little kids think like that. Even Little Bit did some crazy things when she was small. But she wouldn't remember. She refuses to remember anything bad.

My real father was a no-good drunk. The cops hauled him off to jail when I was four. I was scared then too, but I don't remember if that was before or after Krista died. Like I said, Papa was a drunk and hardly ever home. When he was, he always made Mama cry. I hated him for that. And for leaving us alone. They told me later that he died. I said good riddance. He did give me a cowboy gun once. A cap pistol with real caps. I really liked that gun, but they wouldn't let me take it to the orphanage.

Sometimes I wonder if he's really dead. Maybe they lied about that. My old man and old lady lied about a lot of things. They told me Mama died too. And of course they tried to pass off Little Bit as their own. I knew better then, and I know better now, but you won't get her to believe it.

They had to cop to me. I knew it was Grace they had wrapped in that pink blanket. The jerks let me touch her and peek at her face. I was five by then, for crying out loud. Did they think I didn't know my own sister?

I didn't know what they were up to at first. When Mama got sick, Cissy said we'd always be together. "I'll take care of you, Chuckie," she said. "I'll take care of you till Mama gets well, then we'll all be together again."

Lies. Just like everything else is a lie. But I believed her. I believed all the stuff she told me about heaven and God loving us too. For a while.

They took the baby away first. Baby Grace, my little sister. She was red and hot, and coughed a lot. I thought maybe she'd die like Krista, but she didn't. I know she didn't. I been living with her all this time, even though she don't believe it.

Then they came for Mama. They wrapped her in a sheet too, but her face wasn't covered like Krista's. Her eyes were open wide and smiling. She kissed my cheek and told me, "Be a good boy and mind Cissy. Papa and I will be right back." Another lie, of course.

Whew. It's hot in here. This room's a rat hole. I'm gonna bum some beer off the landlady. Don't blow, Joe! Ha.

Back, Jack. Where was I? Oh, yeah. The witch lady with the broom straw hair and bright red lipstick came and hauled us off in a dirty green Edsel. I remember the car. It had hard black seats, and there were tissues and scraps of paper all over the floor.

Cissy told me stories all the way to the orphanage. Of course I didn't know what it was back then. I just remember the cold hard floors, and a long narrow room with metal beds lined up along the walls. Man, it was cold. Made my skin shrivel and stung my eyes. And the smell. Antiseptic and laundry soap combined. I hated that smell.

My old man's hands always smell like antiseptic. Maybe that's why I hate him so much. Maybe not. I have better reasons than that.

It wasn't so bad at the orphanage, after I got used to it anyhow. Cissy stayed with me for awhile. Then she went to sleep in another place, but I saw her every day.

The fat lady with the long black veil scared me. I guess I was scared a lot back then. She was strict, but not mean. Not that I can remember anyway. Then there was Anne. Anne was cool. She tucked me into bed at night when Cissy was too busy, and she gave me an extra turn on the stick horse in the play room.

Once, when I had a cold, she sat me on her lap and fed me honey mixed with lemon juice. I felt better right away, and her lap was almost as comfortable as Cissy's.

Cissy. Oh, God, where is Cissy? Not that God's listening.

Even if he were, he wouldn't tell me. He'd have brought her back a long time ago if he was going to. Or at least given me a clue. But I forgot, God's not real. He's a lie like all the rest, so I guess there's no use asking in the first place.

Man, I need another beer.

When they brought the baby back to the orphanage, I got so excited I turned a cartwheel in the hall. The fat nun told Anne to punish me by making me stand in the corner during supper. She did like she was told, but later she slipped me some crackers and a cold potato. Then she took me to the nursery to see Baby Grace. That's how I know Little Bit isn't Florence. Her name is Grace, and she's been my sister all along.

But I gotta remember Anne is just as conniving as the rest of them. At first I was happy when she came and told me I was going home. She may have said "new home," but if she did I didn't get that part. In my mind, home was Mama and Papa and Cissy and Baby Grace. I knew Krista would never come back. I was only five, but I knew death meant gone for good.

Then the man and lady came. She was much prettier than the witch lady. Her hair was brown, and she had long red nails that shined like glass. And bright red lips and a white-tooth smile. Now I know it was the devil's smile. Back then I thought she was the most beautiful lady I'd ever seen.

Anne brought me to the office. I can see it just like yesterday. Dad was leaning on that big brown desk with his hands in his pockets like he owned the place. He probably did. Probably bought it lock, stock and barrel just so he could call the shots.

Mom sat in the straight-back chair with her legs crossed at the ankle, her nails clicking on the chair arms. When she saw me, she smiled and waited for someone to introduce us. Then she held out her hand. "Come here, Charles," she said to me. "Let me look at you. My, you're a fine young man. Do you like ice cream?"

Man, what a piece of bull. What little kid's going to turn down ice cream?

Before I could tell her I liked chocolate best, they brought in the baby. They carried on like they'd never seen an infant before. Cooing and gooing like a couple of idiots. I never did understand the fuss people make over babies. They don't do anything but eat and sleep and mess their pants.

Anyway, Anne pulled me back a little, so I wouldn't get stepped on, I guess. When they turned around and saw me staring, they sobered up real fast. "This is your new baby sister." They clucked and pulled back the blanket. "Want to see?"

Of course I looked, but it was just Grace. Why did they think she was new? I thought I should explain, so I broke the "don't speak until you're spoken to" rule and said, "Baby Grace was sick, but she's all better now."

There's only one other time I saw a woman look like that. It was when Krista's kitten, Tarzan, peed all over Papa's new socks. He'd left them laying on the bathroom floor. The kitten didn't know better. He must have thought they were softer than the digging box. But when Mama saw (and smelled it too, I'll bet), she went white and mad as murder all at once.

That's how Mom looked when I told them Baby Grace was better. I didn't understand it then. I sure do now.

The man, Dad, turned to Mom and said another thing that puzzled me then: "Don't worry, honey, he'll forget."

Forget. Ha. Did they take me for a jerk? I'll never forget, man. Never. And I'll never forgive them either. Not if I live to be a hundred. But I won't. It's not worth it.

It was Anne who held my hand all the way out to the car. They had the Lincoln then. A long black job, with chrome hub caps and tinted windows. It was Anne who hugged me with tears in her eyes and told me to be a good boy. "Don't fret, Chuckie," she said. "You'll like your new home."

Another lie. What a sucker I was. But I was just a little kid.

I waited a whole week before I asked where Cissy was. When they brought Grace along, I thought Cissy would be waiting at the house. We drove a long time. Now I know it was only two hours, but it seemed like forever back then. I think I fell asleep. The next thing I knew it was morning and I was lying in a strange room in a monster bed that would have held Cissy, Krista, Grace and me all at once.

I could smell coffee and bacon. Sure enough, I found the lady in the kitchen cracking eggs into a pan. Baby Grace was in a cradle by the window. I looked in to see if she was all right, but the lady grabbed me from behind.

"There's my little man!" She squeezed me so hard I nearly wet my pants. Then she turned me around, licked her finger and dug the sleep-sand out of the corners of my eyes.

"There," she clucked, "all clean. Come away now, we don't want to wake the baby."

She led me to the table and lifted me onto one of their cane-back padded chairs. They had them recovered years ago, but then they were a puke-green and white check to match the tablecloth. She tucked a white cloth napkin underneath my chin and went to the stove. Before I could say a word, she was back with a plate piled with bacon, toast and more eggs than a hen can lay in a week.

"Look what Mama's got for you," she said. And then I did wet my pants.

I jumped off the chair and danced around the kitchen, holding the front of my pajama bottoms and peering into every corner. I thought we were playing a game. Mama must be hiding, ready to jump out any minute and yell surprise.

By the time I remembered to ask for the bathroom, my pajamas were soaked and there was a puddle that outdid one of Tarzan's on the kitchen floor.

"Charles! Shame on you." I felt the sting of her hand on my bottom. "You're much too big for that. Go to your room at once and change your clothes. You'll just have to eat your breakfast cold."

My face went hotter than the kitchen stove. I finally found the bathroom just across the hall from the room I'd slept in the night before. When I worked up the courage to go back, I found her sitting at the table, sipping coffee from a china cup and holding Baby Grace.

"Eat your eggs," was all she said to me.

I ate. She was right. The eggs were cold, but they could have been cardboard for all I cared. Because I knew Mama wasn't there. She never would be, or Cissy either. This new mom had been talking about herself. I didn't want to ever eat again.

Chapter
Sixteen

I closed my eyes. This poor tormented soul was not my brother, not the sweet little boy I remembered. My Chuckie was a happy, trusting child, with soft blond curls that were always damp with sweat because he was always running. He never could sit still. He had sticky lollipop kisses and a cock-crow laugh that started deep in his belly and worked its way into your heart.

"That laugh is contagious," Papa would say and tickle him until they were both laughing so hard you couldn't tell one from the other.

My Chuckie had gone on to a better life than I could give him, in a happy Christian home with a mother and father to love him and raise him right.

I heard Aunt Rose sniff quietly as she pressed a tissue into my palm. *Please, God, don't let it be my Chuckie writing this.* But I knew it was. And that meant they'd lied to me as well. Worse, I'd lied to myself and believed the lie. Because I wanted to. Because I couldn't accept the possibility that he might not be happy and secure, like I'd imagined him all these years.

I didn't want to go on reading. I wanted to have tea and toast in Aunt Rose's tidy kitchen, get in my new robin's-egg blue Chevrolet and drive home to my nest in the suburbs. I'd bake chocolate cupcakes for the Halloween party at Libby's school, then fix pork chops and applesauce, one of Jake's favorite dinners. We'd watch *Ozzie and Harriet* or *I Love Lucy,* then say our prayers and dream about the future. The past would stay put in the past, and I would never plead with God to find Chuck and Grace again.

I felt Aunt Rose's arm around my shoulder and smelled her lavender cologne. When I could see, I noticed Uncle Edward's eyes were closed, his lips moving silently, and I knew he was talking to his God. My God too. Although right now it seemed he had deserted me. Just like it seemed he'd deserted the boy whose life was caught between the covers of this dark blue binder.

The crystal anniversary clock on Uncle Edward's mantle chimed the hour. Eleven o'clock. Not much time to finish and get the notebook back to Detective Harman.

There still were so many unanswered questions. I rubbed my aching eyes and turned back to my task. Maybe it would get better. Maybe by some miracle he had worked it through and found a life worth living after all.

But that was not to be. Chuck went on to tell how he'd had nightmares for weeks. He woke up in soiled sheets screaming for me. His mother made him lug the wet linens to the laundry tub and wash them himself by hand. When that didn't work, they promised that if he behaved, they'd take him back to visit me. The bedwetting stopped. But the promise didn't materialize.

To make matters worse, his parents insisted the baby was their own. The DuVals had thought he would forget their excitement when they picked both children up at St. Stephen's. They told him they had wanted a big brother for their baby girl and had brought the infant along for the ride.

"You should be grateful," they insisted. "We've given you a good home."

When Chuckie didn't buy their story and kept repeating, to anyone who would listen, that the baby's real name was Grace, not Florence, the DuVals took more drastic measures.

"One day Mom and Dad told me Baby Grace had died right after the social service people brought her to St. Stephen's. 'So we couldn't have brought your real sister home, now could we?'

" 'Then why does Florence look so much like Grace?' I asked. And they said, 'It's your imagination. All babies look alike.' "

When he was six, he set out to find me and prove them wrong. He stole some money from his mother's purse and took a taxi to the Greyhound depot. But it's a long way from San Diego to Pasadena and St. Stephen's. The bus driver became suspicious of a small boy traveling alone. He called the police, who met them at the next station and drove Chuckie home.

"Dad took me outside behind the garage and paddled my behind. From then on, I kept my hand out of Mom's pocketbook and my opinions to myself. But I couldn't bear to call my sister Florence, so I called her 'Little Bit.' She was small for her age. The nickname fit her, and the folks didn't seem to mind."

The next few pages reflected bits and pieces of his childhood. He seemed to mix one year with another in a jumble of memories—most of them, at least from his perspective, bad.

It broke my heart to realize my brother had grown up unhappy. But aside from the first traumatic months with a new family, I couldn't understand what had driven the sweet, loving little boy I'd known to become so hard and bitter.

Of course I could see his frustration over Baby Grace. I knew very well these people had taken her and Chuckie together. Why would they admit they'd adopted one child and lie about the other? Maybe they were just afraid. Lots of parents were afraid to tell adopted children about their past, afraid they'd lose them unless they kept their backgrounds secret and the records sealed. That was what had stopped me from finding my own siblings. Until now. But as I read on, I had a growing dread that even if my dream were realized, I might not like what I'd found.

* * *

Little Bit was fourteen before I said anything again. We had a party for her on the grounds. Dad set up a canopy and hired a patient of his, a ventriloquist, for entertainment. The caterer brought enough food for a small army. After the cake and punch were cleared away, our parents surprised her with a three-piece band for her and her friends to dance to.

But the band played only Glenn Miller tunes, mixed with Strauss waltzes that would put a night owl to sleep. Our parents and their friends were having a blast, but the kids were bored. Most of the boys had split by nine o'clock, so I made like a big brother and danced with Flo.

When I held her, I almost ducked out myself. It was like dancing with Cissy, Krista and Mama, all rolled into one. Her hair was strawberry blonde, with natural curl, and just long enough to brush her shoulders. She had a sprinkling of freckles across her nose, and the brightest blue eyes I've ever seen.

"What's wrong, Chuck? Have I got cake on my face?"

"Naw. You look pretty tonight, Sis."

She frowned and hung her head. "You're just saying that because you're my brother and you have to be nice to me."

"Oh, come on. Quit fishing for compliments."

"I'm not. Really." I laughed at her, but she wasn't even smiling. "I hate the way I look. Bobbie says I'm cute and Daddy says I'm sweet. I don't want to be any of those. Just once, I want to be beautiful." She took a deep breath and looked right into my eyes. "Sometimes I wish I was somebody else."

I felt like someone had stabbed me in the gut. There were lots of things I could have said. Big brother things, like "Give yourself a chance, you'll be beautiful someday." Instead I heard the words coming from my lips like someone else was in my head spitting them out.

"What if I told you you are?"

"What?"

And then I blew it. I took her upstairs to her room and spilled the whole thing. About Papa and Mama and the orphanage, and how Mom and Dad had been lying about her all these years.

By the time I finished, she was screaming and crying and hitting me with her fists. She couldn't hurt me, of course. Not physically anyway. But then she threw an antique china lamp and splattered it against the bedroom door.

Hell broke loose. The old man tried to kick my rear, but I wasn't six anymore. I was over eighteen and could bench press 240 pounds. I heard the cartilage crunch when my fist made contact with his nose, and I was gone, man. Out of there for real. Didn't even stop to pack my stuff.

That was six years ago and I've only been back once. They said they'd give me another chance, but I couldn't live with the fear in Mom's eyes or the hate I read in the old man's face when he thought I wasn't looking. As for Little Bit, she didn't believe me then, and she don't believe me now.

Well, there it is. The whole stinking deal. Twenty-four years old and I could have had it all, but who needs it? I guess I'll have another beer, then split this scene. Forever.

If God was real maybe he would stop me. Yeah, God, stop me! I dare ya. Just go ahead and try.

Chapter
Seventeen

The camomile tea was cold, but it couldn't quench the fire in the pit of my stomach. If the police had found this notebook, they must have had reason to be in Chuck's room. I couldn't hold back the question any longer.

"Is he dead?"

"Dead!" Aunt Rose looked startled. She turned to Uncle Edward, then back to me, lost for words.

"Oh my stars, Cissy, of course he's not dead."

Uncle Edward cleared his throat. "We told you it was good news, sweetheart. I'm sorry. I thought you'd understand right away."

"Don't you see?" Aunt Rose sounded all excited again. She took my face between her palms, her eyes bright and wet, as if she had a fever. "God stopped him, Cissy. Stopped him sure and true as a lightning bolt. And brought him back into our lives besides."

I felt like someone had wadded up a cotton towel and stuffed it in my head. Then my thoughts began to clear and I understood. But I couldn't believe it. Not until Uncle Edward said it right out loud.

"It's John, Celia. Chuck is our John."

"Or rather, John is Charles. Isn't it wonderful?" Aunt Rose's face was beaming. "I just know that's why I was so taken with that boy."

And I refused to see him. The thought caused my skin to crawl. What if they hadn't found the notebook? He could have walked back out of my life, and because of my stubbornness, I wouldn't have even known he had been there.

Like a sleeper caught in that world between dreams and reality, I couldn't help but wonder if all of this was true. The last I knew, John—no, Chuck—couldn't remember who he was. Temporary amnesia, the doctor had said. So had he suddenly gotten his memory back? Did he tell the police who he was and where he lived?

"The police traced the motorcycle to an artist in Laguna Beach." Uncle Edward answered my unspoken question. "The man remembered seeing Chuck around. They questioned his landlady, and she said he'd been gone for several weeks. When he didn't show up to pay the rent, she stuffed his belongings in a cardboard box and rented the room to someone else."

Aunt Rose shook her head. "Can you imagine? She didn't even report him missing."

Uncle Edward patted her hand. "Now, Rose, it's sad, but people come and go in places like that. She's probably used to packing cardboard boxes."

I shuddered. Uncle Edward's comment reminded me of what dire straits Chuck had fallen into. Somewhere along the line, he had let anger and bitterness overrule common sense. As much as I hated to admit it, my brother was a criminal. Mary Margaret would call him a "hood."

"He's a very mixed-up young man." Aunt Rose handed me another cup of tea. "Here, Cissy. I'll make French toast, and we'll open a jar of strawberry preserves."

Uncle Edward nodded and looked at his watch. "Then we'll take this over to Detective Harman and go by the hospital." He studied my face like it was a map to heaven. "That is, if you want to. We could wait awhile if you're not ready."

I'd wanted this for so long, so why was I so afraid? Deep down, I knew why. God had answered my prayers, but he hadn't done it the way I thought he would. I'd expected a phone call, then a joyous reunion complete with hugs and kisses and a lifetime of happy memories. Who would have ever guessed it would turn out like this?

"Just when you think you've got it all worked out, life takes a left turn and you're lost again." I could hear Papa say that plain as day.

Uncle Edward was waiting for an answer.

"He's my brother," I heard myself say. "Of course we must go."

"I'll take her, Edward. Detective Harman can collect the notebook himself. You know he offered. You've been up too long as it is. Remember what the doctor said."

Uncle Edward looked annoyed. "I know what the doctor said, Rose. I also know how I feel. I'm not too decrepit to handle my responsibilities." He used one crutch for balance and pushed himself to his feet. "Let's eat now, or visiting hours will be over by the time we get there." He kissed Aunt Rose's forehead, to take some of the sting out of his words, I expect. Truth be told, Uncle Edward was not very good at convalescing. He hated "fussing," as he called it, and his usual easy nature had been marred by impatience with "this blamed leg."

Dr. Fob insisted he was healing nicely and they could do more surgery in a month or so, but Uncle Edward didn't want to wait a month. Even though his shoulder throbbed and his left leg still refused to function for more than five minutes without giving out, he wanted to "get on with it." He wanted life to get back to normal.

* * *

It was a blue-sky day, with marshmallow clouds and enough bite in the wind to make me glad I'd worn my new green sweater. Jake had given it to me for my birthday, along with enough money to buy material for a matching skirt.

The roses had finished blooming weeks ago, and the hips were turning brown. I picked one on my way up the path to the courtyard behind the hospital. At my touch, a few wilted pink petals fluttered to the ground and nestled among October leaves that had blown into the garden.

Life is so fragile, I thought. *What's beautiful and blooming one minute dies the next and is carried away by the wind. Hope is like that. And dreams.*

If God sees the sparrow fall, does he keep track of flower petals too? I smiled at the thought. It was a child's question, one Libby would ask and a grown-up would laugh at. I felt like a child, though: innocent as hope, fragile as a dream.

We'd arrived at the hospital less than an hour before. Uncle Edward had insisted on going with us to the fourth floor, where Chuck had been moved the day before. Aunt Rose had tried to talk him into waiting in the lobby. "It's not necessary, Edward. You'll wear yourself out."

But he wouldn't listen, and when we got there, I was glad he hadn't.

The entire floor was in an uproar—police and nurses scurrying around, darting in and out of rooms like a nest of confused mice.

"What's going on?" Uncle Edward stopped Dr. Fob, who was plowing down the hallway shouting orders. Only one nurse seemed to hear a thing he said, and I had to press hard against the wall as she jumped past me to do his bidding.

Dr. Fob jerked his arm away from Uncle Edward's grasp. Then he must have realized who it was.

"Excuse me, Mr. Crandall." He looked Uncle Edward up and down, then steered him toward a chair by the nurses' station. "This is not a good time to be standing in the hall." He nodded in our direction. "You and your family will have to leave. We have a patient missing."

"The boy?"

Dr. Fob nodded. "We finally contacted his parents. One of the nurses told him his father was on the way here. She thought it would cheer him up. Instead he seemed agitated, so she went to call for an okay on a sedative. When she got back to his room, he was gone."

Aunt Rose turned white and had to sit down. I held onto the counter and let the news sink in. He was gone. We had found Chuck and poof, he was gone again. Just like that. I tried to focus on what Dr. Fob was saying.

". . . impossible. He'd only been out of bed twice and his injuries are still serious. He won't get far."

He looked down the hall, where a man in a gray suit blocked the doorway, berating one of the nurses. He was tall, dark and dignified, with a strong chin and a ribbon-thin mustache. He looked familiar somehow, like I'd met him before. But I couldn't think where.

He'd be handsome, I thought, *if it weren't for that ugly scowl.* I couldn't hear his words, but the nurse's face was pale and she seemed to be fighting back tears.

"Excuse me." Dr. Fob caught sight of the two and started down the hall, calling as he went: "Miss Carson, will you please see to the patient in room eight."

The harried nurse moved away and cast him a grateful look over her shoulder.

"Dr. DuVal, isn't it? I'm Brian Fob, your son's physician." He reached the man and deftly grasped his hand. "My office is right this way, sir. We can talk there."

Dr. DuVal.

The man was Chuck's adoptive father.

Chapter
Eighteen

It was quiet on the patio. Most of the commotion was still going on inside the hospital. The police were combing the parking lot out front but hadn't yet ventured into the courtyard or the parklike grounds in back. Dr. Fob had said Chuck's injuries were too debilitating for him to get far and suggested they look in vacant rooms or unlocked cars in the lot.

When I left, Uncle Edward was still pumping the officer in charge for information. Aunt Rose was, I suspected, still in the ladies' room trying to control her tears.

I felt a pang of guilt. I should have been comforting her instead of hiding out in the gardens. She had been the one closest to "John"; I hadn't seen my brother in almost twenty years, and the Charles of the dark-blue notebook was someone I had never known.

I'd stayed long enough, though, to overhear the head nurse tell Uncle Edward that the police had issued a warrant for Chuck's arrest on theft charges for the stolen motorcycle. Of course, if that same nurse hadn't told him his father was coming, he'd have been under police guard with no chance of escape.

I'd been overwhelmed with the need to escape myself, so I had hurried out the double doors and took the back stairs three at a time until I ran out of breath in the rose garden. Jake would have been impressed.

The bench I sat on was pink adobe to match the bricks in the patio. The gravel path continued a few more yards through a patch of grass and into a stand of young oak trees. The sun splashed leafy shadows on the lawn and warmed my hair. I closed my eyes and tried to soak up the warmth, but I still felt cold down deep inside where the sun couldn't reach.

I tried to pray, but found myself daydreaming instead. What if we'd all stayed together—Chuckie, Baby Grace and I? Would Mama have recovered and come home to do her job?

The thought startled me, but I realized I was angry. With Mama for going off into her head instead of facing her responsibilities, and with God for allowing her to do it. Didn't he know we were all too young to be without a mother? True, he had given me Aunt Rose and Uncle Edward. And after a few hard months, my life had turned out for the good. But what about Chuck? Why couldn't he have adjusted better to his new home or, better yet, come to live with Aunt Rose and Uncle Edward too?

Foolish speculation. And it wouldn't do a speck of good.

* * *

I heard voices, then footsteps on the gravel path. Two policemen and a hospital security guard were moving slowly toward the courtyard, pawing through bushes and peering behind every tree.

I moved quickly over the gravel path and into the stand of oaks. I could hear water trickling nearby. We were in the foothills, up against Mount Baldy, where any one of a thousand streams could run into a creek.

I knew I should go back, find Aunt Rose and let the police do their job. Sister Veronica had been right, I thought, and Mrs. Granger too. I had no business in this boy's life. His father was there, and surely he wouldn't want us to interfere.

The path ended. But instead of turning back, I moved toward the sound of the water. It drew me to a clearing where a clump of weeds and tall grasses blocked access to the creek. I could see the cool, fresh water rushing over scoured-smooth stones. It ran fastest where the shallow channel narrowed abruptly, bubbled around a fallen sapling, then flowed into a wider pool where it seemed to rest, deep and still, before continuing its winding course.

Suddenly I felt thirsty, like I hadn't had a drop to drink in days. I looked around and found a fallen branch from one of the young trees. The only way to water was through the weeds, and the last thing I wanted was to run into a snake. I hated snakes—spiders too—and if I had stopped to think about it, I would have turned around and gone back to the hospital. I could have had water from the drinking fountain, or a Coke from the cafeteria, but that never entered my head until later.

* * *

They said I never screamed. The policemen said they hadn't heard a sound. They didn't even know I was there until they spotted my sweater caught on a thistle bush and saw it move.

When I thought about it later, I told Aunt Rose, "It's hard to scream when your heart's in your throat." We both laughed, but it wasn't funny at the time.

* * *

I picked up the stick and beat a path through the weeds and grass. I'd almost made it to the water when I scared up a small green garden snake. It spit at me, then darted away. I jumped, of course, and landed against something solid. I tried to get my balance, but something else caught my ankle and jerked, and down I went, landing on my hands and knees. The air left my lungs with a whoosh.

When I could breathe again, I found myself face to face with a bloody corpse. At least that's what I thought at the time.

The hand that had grabbed my ankle lay limp and still beside the death-white body. His eyes were closed, and blood seeped from a freshly opened wound on his forehead. The bandage around his head and the shoulder of his hospital gown were soaked with it.

I couldn't have run if I'd wanted to, so I pressed my fingers against his neck to see if he had a pulse. His skin felt cold and damp, like Jake's when he finished lifting weights. He always took a shower to cool off, but he couldn't quit sweating and his skin felt clammy for hours.

When I touched him, he moaned and opened his eyes. Papa's eyes. And a fat, pink, wormlike scar, older than the rest, stretched across his cheek.

"Oh Chuck, I love you." Had I said it aloud? I hoped so.

Chuck moaned again and closed his eyes. Then the police were there, and Dr. Fob, and two orderlies with a stretcher. Strong hands helped me up, gripped my elbow and led me back to the path.

"Are you all right?"

I nodded yes. The hands released me and moved away.

"Easy, you idiots! Slow down or you'll drop him. Come this way, to your left. Now set him down."

Not Dr. Fob. The voice was deeper, more abrupt.

"His pulse is strong. Take him back to his room, please. I'll be right there." That was Dr. Fob.

I watched the scene unfold in a blur of motion and sound. The orderlies pushed by me, balancing the stretcher between them like a basket of eggs.

"No disrespect intended, doctor, but the boy is still my patient. Why don't you go to my office? Miss Carson will get you a cup of coffee."

The voice turned toward me. Gentle fingers probed my face

and arms. "Mrs. Freeman?" He snapped his fingers in front of my eyes. I blinked, and it must have satisfied him. "Here's your aunt." He looked away from me and went on. "Take her on up to the fourth floor, Mrs. Crandall. I'll have one of the nurses look at her. Then you should all go home. There's nothing you can do for him right now."

Aunt Rose put her arms around me and led me down the path toward the courtyard. The men hurried past us.

"Hold on, Fob. Who in blazes is that woman, and what was she doing with my son? I want some answers and I want them now."

I couldn't hear Dr. Fob's quiet reply, but I knew one thing for certain: I did not think very highly of Dr. Robert DuVal. From what I'd seen and heard today, I had to agree with Chuck: his father was a jerk.

Chapter
Nineteen

***

The next few hours were a blur. Uncle Edward must have
called Jake, because he was waiting for me when I pulled into
the driveway. The long drive home had done little to settle my
spirit, and I felt only a numb relief when he pulled me into his
arms.

He insisted I go to bed early, but as tired as I was, I heard
every sound: Libby's excited chatter over the TV dinners Jake
had fixed, her protests when he declared an early bedtime. I
wanted to jump in and tell him she could stay up until eight
on weeknights, but I didn't have the energy to move.

I heard the snap of the television dial and listened to the
comedy of errors as Ozzie missed yet another dinner party and
Harriet tried to cover for him with her quiet excuses and in-
evitable smile. I felt a mild disappointment that David and
Ricky weren't in that episode, then annoyance as Eve Arden
and Gale Gordon traded barbs on *Our Miss Brooks* and kept
Jake laughing.

The TV snapped off, and Jake crept quietly into bed. I rolled
onto my back and pretended to be asleep. I didn't know what
Uncle Edward had told him, but he hadn't asked for details. *It's
just as well,* I thought as his lips brushed my forehead. *I don't*

want to talk about it right now.

* * *

Aunt Rose called several times throughout the week—in the evening when Jake was home to answer the phone. He related her news that Chuck was back in bed and it didn't look like his attempt to escape had caused any further damage. Nothing physical anyway.

The next Wednesday she told us Dr. DuVal had agreed to let her and Uncle Edward see him. "Tell her Charles remembered me and seemed glad for the company," she told Jake. "But he couldn't bear to look at Edward, so we left again right away."

* * *

By Thursday, I knew I had to get out of the house or go crazy. Some of my old energy had returned, and I was feeling restless.

Mr. Johnson sounded relieved when I phoned to say I'd be in by ten. "I'm afraid there's a mountain of papers on your desk," he apologized. "I hope you don't think we're taking advantage of you, but it feels great to get home before seven every night."

I dug into the pile with relish, glad to have something besides Chuck to turn my mind to. Three hours later, I realized two things: the stack of letters and file folders had diminished by half, and in spite of the fact that I no longer needed to search for my brother and sister, I was going to keep this job.

* * *

I managed to finish Libby's good-fairy costume the day before Halloween. I had gathered several yards of netting and basted it around the skirt of her old white nylon dress. The bodice and waist were too snug and the skirt too short, but with the netting and some odds and ends of lace, it would do. As her father assured her a dozen times, she would look like a dream at her school party.

She had cut the cardboard star herself, covered it with foil and glued it to the end of the baton Mary Margaret had given her for Christmas. I thought a broom handle would have served better.

"It's way too long, Mother," Libby said, looking exasperated, "and we'd have to cut off the straw part."

Jake wandered around the kitchen peering into cupboards and drawers. "I have a tire iron she can use," he volunteered.

"Daddy!"

He grinned from behind the lid to the cookie jar. "Jake, please stop prowling. You can't have any candy until tomorrow night after the children have gone."

"Yeah, Dad. Anyway, Mama hid it where you'll never find it," she taunted. "Never in a million years!"

"Wanna bet?" Jake's grin grew wider, and the search was on, with Libby's gasps and squeals guiding him like a game of Hot Potato, Cold Potato.

When he got to the cupboard above the Frigidaire, Libby was practically rolling on the floor. "No, not there. She'd never hide it there."

With a smile of triumph, he dug behind a row of canning jars and pulled out the basket of penny candies. Each little packet held three candies and a piece of bubble gum. I'd done them up in cellophane tied with white string. There were candy apples too, of course, for Dotty's brood and a few other friends.

Jake exclaimed that he would give up his find for the price of one candy apple. Libby agreed it was a fair trade, especially when he shared the treat with her.

"Jake! She'll be sick. They already had candy and cupcakes at school, and she'll have a sackful by tomorrow night."

My protests were met with sticky grins from both culprits. Jake curled his hands into claws, crouched and stalked in my direction. "Come here, my pretty," he teased. "I have a treat for you."

I threw my hands up in defeat and ran. I could hear Libby's laughter as Jake caught me in the hall and planted sticky kisses all over my face.

He held me for a moment. The spark of mischief in his eyes flared into a different kind of fire, and reluctantly, he let me go.

I looked at Libby, still watching from the kitchen doorway, then back to Jake, whose eyes had followed mine. I licked my lips and thought how that caramel was the sweetest thing I'd tasted in a long, long time.

* * *

Mary Margaret telephoned on Friday morning, right after her shift at Douglas. "I can't understand why Daddy keeps going back to that hospital," she said. "You'd think he'd want to stay away from that place, not to mention that horrible kid." She caught herself. "Sorry, Celia," she went on, "but it's true. Anyway, if you ask me, Mother and Daddy would be better off to leave it alone. The boy's family is there now; let them deal with it."

Well, I thought, *I didn't ask you.* But still, I had to admit that some of what she said was true. Uncle Edward should be home resting and getting his strength back. And Aunt Rose had her hands full enough as it was. In a way, the whole situation might be better resolved if the two of them just left it to the others.

Yet I knew that none of us could just let it go. After seeing his face, even with the scars and bruises that had still not healed, I knew without a doubt the boy in that hospital was Chuck.

Boy? In the notebook he had said that he was twenty-four. That meant Grace would be nineteen. No, she would have turned twenty last June. And Chuck would turn twenty-five two months from now on Christmas Eve.

Mary Margaret finally quit ranting and said she had to go to bed. The phone rang again immediately. It was Dotty, asking what time we'd all get together for trick-or-treating that night.

"The little ones have to go before dark," she reminded me. "We can eat afterward, then let Sam and Jake take the other three. I'll bring the salad and the bread."

She hung up a few minutes later, and I went on with preparations for the evening. But even then I knew that sooner or later Aunt Rose would call and ask for me.

* * *

Sam and Dotty took their children home at nine. David insisted on keeping his pirate's eye patch on and tripped all over himself trying to lug his pillowcase of candy down the steps. Rachel led the sleepy twins, each clutching a bag of candy and holding up the tail to a kitty costume. Sam carried little Zeke, who had fallen asleep on the floor, his face smeared with chocolate from the two Hershey bars his parents had forbidden him to eat.

I sighed and closed the door after them. "It's a good thing it's Friday night. They'll all have stomachaches tomorrow." Over Libby's protests, I stowed her cache of candy on top of the fridge.

"Two pieces a day, sweetheart," I said firmly. "You know the rules."

I kissed the top of her hair and made a mental note to wash it in the morning. She'd talked me into letting her get a bob. Jake had been disappointed but told her she looked beautiful, of course. I had to admit it was easier to keep clean and brushed.

"She'll have the candy gone by Monday." Jake smiled as he shut the kitchen window and locked the back door.

"With your help," I countered.

We both knew "the rules" were only a formality. It was easier to give in to Libby's wheedling and let her finish it off. Besides, there was plenty of chewing gum and fruit to offset the sweets.

Jake put his arm around my waist and led me to our bedroom. "We spoil her, don't we?" He chuckled, then grew quiet as he hung up his shirt and draped his pants across the cedar chest. I changed in the bathroom. When I came back into the room, he was lying on his back, both arms tucked behind his head, staring at the ceiling. His eyes turned toward me just before I switched off the light; I could feel them follow me from the doorway to the bed.

The covers were already pulled back. I fluffed my pillow and settled in, pulling the covers up to my chest and tucking my arms underneath. I felt suddenly cold and wanted to snuggle, but Jake didn't move.

"Celia, we have to talk."

Chapter
Twenty

"Celia, this won't just go away, you know."

I shook my head and realized he probably couldn't see the movement. "I can't talk about this, Jake. Not yet. I'm still mixed up about so much of it."

He sighed and turned toward me. "That's why you need to spill it, babe. I can't help you if you won't let me in."

Let him in? Had I been shutting him out? I'd tried so hard to act normal ever since we found Chuck. I listened to his talk about the shop, even asked questions and offered to help him set up. I'd kept up with the house, cooked a pot roast, made candy apples and baked his favorite chocolate cake. Wasn't that enough?

I knew it wasn't. I shifted toward him and stroked his upper arm. He turned again and drew me with him, my head tucked into the hollow of his shoulder. I felt his lips against my hair and knew he was waiting for me to begin.

"I don't know where to start."

"He's your brother, Celia. You've been searching for him all these years. He's not going to disappear again just because you don't like what you found."

He said it gently, but I felt my body stiffen in response. Jake was right. I'd been pretending like the whole thing had never happened. The notebook, the hospital, the tormented person who'd turned out to be my brother—they were all part of some nightmare. If I just kept my eyes closed and waited it out, or buried myself in work, I'd wake up and it would all be over.

"Oh, Jake," I whispered. "What are we going to do?"

His arm tightened around me. "We'll get through this, babe. A day at a time if we have to, but we'll sort it out."

He kissed my forehead and my chin, then his lips brushed feather-light against my own. I felt the sticky dampness on his cheek and knew it wasn't from a caramel apple.

* * *

Aunt Rose called at ten o'clock Saturday morning.

"He wants to see you, Cissy," she said. "Why don't you and Jake come for dinner tomorrow, and we'll all go over around seven?"

It was more than a suggestion. I didn't have the nerve to turn her down. Besides, Jake had been right: putting it off wouldn't make it any easier. I had to face the situation. For better or worse, he was my brother and I knew I'd always love him, no matter who or what he had become.

Somehow I managed to make it through the day. Jake washed the car and cleaned out the incinerator, while I sewed a pair of pedal pushers for Libby. Sam and Dotty had taken Libby with them to Knotts Berry Farm to celebrate Rachel's birthday, and it was a good time for me to get a head start on Christmas gifts.

Around noon, I took a break and fixed some tuna sandwiches.

"What time is dinner tomorrow night?" Jake snatched the mayonnaise jar and added another dollop to his bread.

"Aunt Rose said around five." I finished chopping a sweet pickle, added a drop of mustard to the mix, and put the sandwiches together. Then I stopped. "Do you think he hates me?"

"Why should he hate you, Celia?" He reached across the table and squeezed my hand. "Maybe your brother hasn't had the ideal life, but he can't blame that on you. Don't be so hard on yourself." He finished one sandwich in four bites and started on the other.

"Besides, you haven't seen him since he was a little kid, and little kids change. How do you know he wouldn't have turned out the same if you had all stayed together? From what you told me about the notebook, he wasn't so hot on his real father either."

My own lunch tasted bitter and my mouth was dry. I pushed the plate to Jake.

"Are you sure?"

I nodded. "I guess I'm just too nervous to eat."

"Then it's a good thing we're getting this over with tomorrow." He washed down the last bite of sandwich with a glass of milk. "Otherwise, I'd be fat as a hog by Christmas."

He set his napkin on the empty plate and kissed me on the forehead. "Gotta wax the car," he said, and I heard the kitchen window rattle as the back door slammed.

If Libby had done that, he'd have yelled at her but good. I shook my head. "Men, they're nothing but little boys in a grown-up body." Dotty had said that more times than I could count.

Still, in a way I guessed Jake was right. Chuck sure did have a different view of Papa than I did. Why did he only remember the bad things? The father I remembered drank sometimes and sometimes came home late, but he always said, "I love you, pumpkins," and dandled Chuckie on his knee.

He loved our mama too, even though it didn't always show. And she loved him. Enough to follow him to kingdom come and back if she had to.

But look where it got her.

I set aside the dishes and tried to get back to my sewing. But I stitched a back and front together instead of two backs and had to rip the seam apart. By the time I was ready to try again, I heard the Levis' car in the drive and had to hurriedly bury Libby's unfinished gift deep in my sewing basket.

Libby was sick in the night. Dot had warned me she and Rachel had eaten too much rhubarb pie. "They must have devoured an entire pie between them, and a chicken dinner besides. If I were you, Celia, I'd dose her good with milk of magnesia before she goes to bed."

But Libby swore she'd lose her dinner at the sight of the blue and white bottle, so I gave in and let her go without. It turned out she kept us both up all night, which I thought later was just as well. The dreams she woke me from weren't pleasant ones.

Chapter
Twenty-one

Jake fished out a five-dollar bill to pay for gasoline on the way to Uncle Edward's. When they only gave him back a dollar in change, he flinched and stuffed it in his wallet.

As I sat waiting for the attendants to finish wiping the windows clean, my mind flashed back to the morning's sermon. "Just trust in God when you can't see the light, and he'll show you the way," Pastor Willis had said.

I do trust you, Lord, I prayed silently, *but I surely don't see the way.*

"Celia, will you relax? You're so stiff you won't be able to move by the time we get there."

I looked down at my hands. The knuckles of my right hand were white from gripping the door handle; my left hand was balled into a fist. I buried it in the folds of my new plaid skirt.

"I shouldn't have worn this, it really is too young for me. Libby says it would look better with a petticoat. What do you think?"

"I think I'm going to listen to the radio," he said and turned the knob on the dash.

"What on earth is that?"

Jake turned up the volume. "It's called rhythm and blues,

woman," he shouted over the wailing of a saxophone. "Where have you been? It's practically all they play anymore."

I wanted to tell him I'd been running his home and raising his daughter, but I didn't have the energy to compete with the noise coming from the radio. Anyway, there was no need to snap at Jake; he was just trying to cheer me up. I closed my eyes, laid my head back on the seat and allowed the music to wash over me.

Jake let the radio blare until we pulled into Uncle Edward's driveway.

*　*　*

Chuck was sitting up when we got to the hospital. His eyes were slits in his scar-puffed face, but they were open, and I thought I saw the hint of a smile around the corners of his mouth.

"You're not Cissy."

I could barely understand the mumbling. One of his bottom teeth was broken, and the top two front ones were completely missing. Even while I struggled to take in his words, my mind flashed a picture of Chuckie at five. Just before he'd left St. Stephen's, his top two baby teeth had fallen out. Anne had gasped and dragged him to the infirmary, but Sister Veronica had shrugged and said, "It's only natural. He must have cut them early."

Now everyone in the room was standing still as stone, waiting for my reaction.

Everyone, that is, except the young man propped up on pillows in the hospital bed. His hands were shaking beneath the sheet. "You're not Cissy," he said again. This time a gap-tooth grin appeared. "You're Mama, come back to haunt me."

I sat down on the bed, wrapped my arms around my brother, cast and all, and cried.

I don't know how long we stayed like that. Once a nurse

brought in a glass of juice and two white pills the size of almonds. "Horse pills," Papa would have called them. Chuck waved them away. The girl shrugged, set them on the bedside tray and backed out of the room. Only then did I notice that the others had left as well. We were alone for the first time in over twenty years.

I admit, I did most of the talking. I could tell it was difficult for him to speak, and he seemed content to listen. He stopped me only once. When I told him how Uncle Edward had tried to find both him and Grace after they'd found me, he took hold of my arm. His grip was surprisingly strong for a man in his condition, and for a moment I was afraid. But then I saw the pain in his eyes and heard the quiver in his voice.

"Why . . . why didn't you come too? It would have been so much easier."

Why indeed? How could I make him understand, when I really didn't understand it all myself?

They had tricked me, to be sure. Anne had pretended there were chores for me to do in the day room, and they'd squirreled the little ones away. They didn't want a fuss, I suppose. How could I say, "Your new family didn't want me"? That I was too old and that they had wanted children they could raise to suit themselves?

I should have told him they had his best interest at heart. That they had fully intended to give him and Baby Grace a good home. I should have said God was in control then, too—the same God who had brought us back together now. But I didn't think of any of that. So we stayed silent for a while until Chuck withdrew his hand and closed his eyes.

The door swung open, and Dr. DuVal stood at the foot of the bed. "You've tired him," he said. "I must ask you to leave now."

Chuck's eyes flashed open. Wider than I had seen them all afternoon.

I squeezed his hand. "Your father's right," I said, "you need to rest. I'll be back, I promise." I smiled and kissed him on the cheek. He smelled of liniment and bandages and a sweet summer scent I couldn't put my finger on.

I left him glaring at his father and joined Aunt Rose and Jake in the waiting room. It seemed strange to see them sitting there, Aunt Rose thumbing through a *Reader's Digest* and Jake poring over a *Popular Science* magazine he'd brought along. Somehow they looked like strangers—people I'd never met, in a life I'd never lived. I rubbed my eyes and rolled my shoulders back to get the kinks out.

Jake looked up, and the spell was broken. "Well, we thought you'd taken up residence in there."

Aunt Rose set the magazine aside and stood. I could see the concern in her eyes, but she didn't voice the questions I knew she must be dying to ask. "Dr. Fob found a place for Edward to lie down," she said. "We didn't want to rush you."

I felt a twinge of guilt, then brushed it away. They had wanted this as much as I did, and Uncle Edward had insisted on coming along.

Jake stood and stretched, then walked over and took my hand. "Let's go home, babe. We can talk about it when you're ready."

I flashed him a grateful smile and let him lead me down the hall and out into the cool night air.

* * *

There was something in the room. Something trapped and frightened and dangerous, like an animal that would do anything to escape. Anything at all. I'd heard how a coyote or a fox would even chew off its own paw to escape a hunter's trap. My heart pounded, not so much with fear as a desperate need to help the thing. It was injured—I knew that without a doubt—bleeding and in pain.

I had to do something, but try as I might I could not move through the tarlike fog that swirled around the doorway. My legs were lead weights keeping me bolted to the ground. My arms flailed at the thick black air, disturbing it just enough to allow a glimpse of orange light at the back of the room.

Lord, help me, I cried aloud. *I have to save him, I have to.* The fog became smoke; the flickering light, flames. Now I stood outside the house and watched it burn, unable to go any closer because of the intense heat.

The smoke cleared for an instant, and I saw a face pressed up against the bedroom window. A child's face. A boy about four or five years old. He glared at me through the darkening glass, a look that spoke volumes about the fear and anger in his heart.

Suddenly everything grew bright, and the air vibrated with the sound of an explosion. I closed my eyes against the blinding light. When I dared to look, the house was gone, except for the room where the child was trapped. I searched the window frantically, but there was no sign of the boy.

In the hot, dry silence I heard a siren growing louder and closer. It was too late.

"Celia, come on, wake up. It's seven o'clock. You overslept, and Libby will be late for school." Jake's hand shook my shoulder and roused me from my dream.

My head still felt like I was in a fog, my limbs heavy with sleep. I swung my legs over the side of the bed to show Jake I was awake. The action must have satisfied him, because he moved back to face the mirror on my dressing table, knotting his tie and smoothing back his hair.

"I have an appointment with the bank today. To close on the loan. There shouldn't be any problem, but I can't believe how nervous I am." His eyes met mine in the mirror, and he offered a lopsided grin.

I thought how handsome he looked. A few short flakes of gray dotted his sideburns and crawled along the stubble on the back of his neck. But for the most part, he still looked young. More like Chuck's age than ten years older.

Chuck.

I tucked my feet into the fuzzy pink bedroom slippers Libby had given me for my birthday and prayed to God that the dream was wrong.

It wasn't too late.

Chapter
Twenty-two

Back in September, a young actor named James Dean had been killed in a fiery car crash up on Highway 46. It had made my skin crawl when I read it in the Sunday *Times*. He was driving one of those fancy sports cars, and I guess he had been going way too fast. "Reckless and daring," people said about him.

"Careless and stupid," was Jake's verdict. "What a waste!" Somehow I got the impression he meant the car as much as the young man's life.

"It's awful," I remember telling him. "He was the same age as Chuck."

In late November, the Temple Theater had a showing of James Dean's latest movie, *Rebel Without a Cause*. Everyone was talking about it.

"You won't like it," Mary Margaret insisted. "The boys are punks, the girl is a little tramp, and the parents are—"

"M!"

"Well, it's a ridiculous movie. If you ask me, it'll just put ideas into kids' heads. They can get into trouble enough on their own. Look at your brother."

At least she was finally referring to him as my brother instead of "that dirty little maggot who tried to kill Daddy." She'd had to switch from "juvenile delinquent" when we found out he was twenty-four and not nineteen.

In spite of her opinion, she came and sat with Libby so Jake and I could go to the movie. She even baked a chocolate cake while we were gone.

"Libby helped," she said with a shrug when I thanked her. "I'll take my piece home and eat it tomorrow. Chocolate gives me nightmares."

I sighed and shut the door behind her.

She had finally broken down and bought a brand-new Hudson, a custom Wasp sedan. "The way things are changing, it's impossible to get around without a car," she said, like I hadn't been telling her that for years. "Anyway, how could I pass up something with a name like Wasp?"

While Mary Margaret gunned her engine and pulled out of the driveway, I set a slice of cake in front of Jake. "You know," I said, "that boy, Jim, was a lot like Chuck. He got into trouble because he thought his parents didn't understand him."

Jake scowled. "All kids think that at one time or another. It's called growing pains. They should have taught him some respect. Anyway, the boy in the movie wasn't adopted."

"I know. But doesn't that make Chuck's situation that much more understandable?"

"How can you say that, Celia? Even Chuck admits he should have done things different when he made the choice to leave. He was nineteen, for Pete's sake. He could have gotten out of there by going to college. Even after he busted his old man in the kisser, they offered to take him back and pay his way."

"Jake Freeman, when did you ever learn to talk like that?" I put my finger to my lips and pointed toward Libby's bedroom. "Remember, the walls have ears," I whispered. "I'm not trying to make excuses for his behavior, just—"

"You could have fooled me." Jake grinned and ruffled my

hair. "You're awfully cute when you're riled. But for once I have to agree with Mary Margaret. It was a stupid movie." He yawned. "Man, I'm beat. And we have to get up for church tomorrow." He handed me his empty plate and kissed me good-night.

I put our plates and glasses to soak in the sink, then changed my mind, added a dollop of Joy and did them up. I got a lot of my thinking done with my arms buried up to the elbows in suds. The warm water calmed my nerves.

Was I really trying to make excuses for Chuck? Certainly there could be no excuse for drinking too much or stealing. And Jake was right: Chuck admitted that some of his behavior had been rash.

Robert DuVal had stated his case the last time we saw him. "You can't expect a five-year-old to move from one family to another without some adjustments," he'd said. "We did our best to help him, but look where it got us. The boy made his own decisions; he'll just have to live with the consequences."

Chuck's feelings toward his parents hadn't softened any. I could see why. His father was a hard man. Hard and proud.

Dr. DuVal had made the remarks during a "family" meeting, with Aunt Rose, Uncle Edward and me in the room "as witnesses." Chuck's mother had declined to attend. "This entire situation has upset her terribly. She's been under considerable stress, and we thought it best that she wait to see you when you're a little more stable," Dr. DuVal had said as he stood stiff as Hitler at the foot of Chuck's bed. The rest of us sat awkwardly in chairs that had been squeezed into the tiny room.

The doctor made it clear he would help Chuck, but only on his own terms. Chuck would have to shape up, take his medicine with the law and prove he wanted to be an upstanding citizen. Then the DuVals would take him back, pay his hospital bills and help him find a decent job.

The final stipulation was that Chuck must leave his sister Florence alone. "She's an honor student at USC and happy there. Under no condition are you to bother her with your foolish notions. She told you once that she doesn't believe you, and there it stands."

He glared at us like we were the devil's demons. It was obvious the edict applied to everyone in the room.

"Do I make myself clear?"

"Perfectly." Chuck's voice was stronger than it had been since the accident.

When visiting hours were over, Dr. DuVal drew me aside. "You won't help him by stirring the whole thing up," he cautioned. "The sooner you both understand that your sister died at St. Stephen's, the sooner Chuck will get well. Until then, I fear for his sanity." He raised his eyebrows. "And perhaps yours as well."

Uncle Edward had been livid. He'd already contacted St. Stephen's, where a slightly rattled Mother Superior insisted there had never been a death in that building, infant or otherwise. And no, Sister Veronica could not be reached; she'd gone on to her reward last spring. "At St. Luke's Hospital," she'd been quick to point out. "You may check if you like."

St. Stephen's had ceased to be an orphanage long ago, before the war. Now the old building was used as a convent, and even that was in danger of shutting down. "Most of the records from that period have been removed," the woman admitted, "but I would certainly have known of anything as serious as a death." Uncle Edward wanted to approach Dr. DuVal with that information now. "And cram it down his throat," he'd added.

"Edward!" Aunt Rose had been alarmed at the venom in his tone.

He apologized immediately. "I'm sorry, Rosie. Please forgive me. It's just that this deception makes me so angry. There must be something we can do about it."

"It's not me you need to ask forgiveness from, dear," she said gently, then sighed. "You're right. There must be a way to unmask this situation once and for all, but we don't want to hurt Grace, or her parents." She nudged Uncle Edward back into his seat. "Those people are hurting too, you know that. Otherwise they wouldn't be so bent on protecting themselves. They're afraid."

She turned and put her arm around my shoulder. "God has a plan, sweetheart, one that will work out for the good of all of us."

I nodded, but at the time I wasn't sure it was true. How could this ever be solved without someone getting hurt? Our lives were already upside down. Maybe Robert DuVal was right. Maybe we should just leave well enough alone and let Grace go on being Florence.

Yet I knew in my heart that Chuck at least would never let it go. *And,* I thought as I turned out the kitchen light and headed to bed myself, *neither can I.*

Chapter
Twenty-three

Anne Marie came home for good around the end of November. Jake and I took Libby to the Freemans' on December 5, to celebrate Davy's—or rather, Dave's—and Amy's eighteenth birthdays.

Except for a few tiny lines around her eyes and mouth, Anne Marie looked the same. She'd turned thirty-one last June but could pass for twenty with her petite figure and huge brown eyes.

It was the first I'd seen her since her husband died. She looked fragile, like a china doll that might break if held too tight. I was surprised at the strength in her arms when she returned my hug.

"Celia, it's so good to see you!" Her voice was steady and her enthusiasm genuine. I pushed her to arm's length and looked into her eyes—not awash with hurt like I'd expected, but filled with genuine peace.

"Anne Marie, you look wonderful. I'm so glad you're home. You'll have to tell us all about your plans."

She hugged her brother next, and I watched Jake's eyes lighten with relief. We'd both been worried about her recovery. Now it seemed she'd handled her grieving well.

She released Jake, tucked her arm through mine and led us toward the kitchen, where Ma Freeman bent over the same dilapidated white stove she'd had since 1932.

"My Jake!" she cried and smothered him in a hug. "Where's the baby?"

Without waiting for an answer, she turned to me. "Ah, Celia, let me look at you." She kissed my cheek and spun me around. "I can see my boy is taking good care of you, even if you are a bit skinny," she sighed, "just like Anne Marie. You girls must not eat a thing."

She ran a hand across her own ample stomach and vowed, "Now that Anne's home, I can fatten her up a little. But you," she added, shaking her head, "I just don't see you enough."

She turned and slapped Jake's hand as he reached for the lid to the cooking pot. "Out! Your father and Dave are out back working on that jalopy of his. A waste of time and money if you ask me, which of course they don't."

Libby came racing through the back door, grinning and holding out a piece of shocking pink angora. "Look, Mom! Just look what Davy gave me." She still called her uncle "Davy," and he never corrected her, although he'd have had a fit if one of us tried it.

"What on earth?" It looked like a scrap of someone's sweater.

"It's a mirror warmer. Davy's girlfriend—no, ex-girlfriend—gave it to him. They broke up and he doesn't want it anymore. Isn't that boss?"

"Libby, don't talk—"

"Libby Jane, come kiss your grandma. Oh, just look at you." Ma Freeman pinched Libby's cheeks, then promptly reached for a tissue from her apron pocket. "Land sakes, child, you have grease all over your face. And put that thing away, it looks like somebody dyed a rat and sewed it head to tail."

Libby submitted to the scrubbing with a good-natured grin.

"But Grandma, Davy gave it to me. I don't have a car, so I'm going to hang it on the mirror in my room."

I had to smile. She'd been enamored of her Uncle Dave since she was a skinny eight-year-old and he a gangling high-school freshman. Once at a Thanksgiving dinner she had declared, "I'm going to marry Davy when I grow up." We all smiled. All except for Davy, who turned beet-red and asked to be excused. His rejection didn't faze Libby a bit. She simply assumed a patient and, I thought, patronizing smile and whispered, "Well, I am. Just wait and see." Her infatuation had only deepened with time, and I wondered if we shouldn't be concerned.

"Oh, Celia, she's beautiful." Anne Marie's gasp broke into my thoughts. "And so grown up!" She took Libby's hands and drew her gently away from Ma Freeman's scouring.

Libby looked down at her shoes, then raised her head to look at Anne with a shy, delighted smile. Their eyes met, and I was startled by the connection that flowed between them like an electric current. I thought the resemblance was uncanny. When I spoke to Jake about it later, he said I was crazy.

"Don't be silly, Celia. Libby's almost a redhead. Anne Marie is dark. They don't look a thing alike."

But it was there. I could see it in their faces: high cheekbones, the same slightly pointed chin. They were both small-boned, although Libby would probably be taller. In any case, when I watched them get reacquainted that day, I knew that Libby had found in her Aunt Anne a lifelong friend.

"Anne Marie, go fetch your sister," Ma Freeman instructed. "She's been primping long enough. The others will be here any minute." As usual, she didn't specify which sister, but I assumed she must mean Amy, since she and Dave were the only ones left at home.

"Sit, Celia. I have to stir the sauce." She pushed me toward the huge kitchen table that had been extended with all three leaves.

The sweet-spice smells of spaghetti sauce and garlic made my stomach rumble, and I realized I hadn't eaten a thing since the night before. I'd fixed bacon and eggs for Libby and Jake that morning, but I'd been too busy wrapping birthday gifts and icing the twins' cake to eat myself.

Ma Freeman had always been a wonderful cook. When the kids were small, she'd had to make do with whatever she had on hand. When I asked for a recipe, it was always "a pinch of this and a handful of that." I never could duplicate her wonderful stews and sauces, so I made up my own or relied on Aunt Rose's tried and true cuisine. I'd been too young to learn much from Mama, except how to cook fresh green beans and make Grandma Eva's enchiladas. Still, Jake seemed to like my cooking. At least he never complained, and once in a while he'd smile and say, "Great dinner, babe."

"I'll set the table," I said and grabbed a pile of dishes from the cupboard above the sink. I was appalled by the rusty basin. Jake had given it a new coat of enamel a few years back, but it had obviously worn off. I had to push back a stab of resentment toward Jake's father. I knew he wasn't a lazy man and he'd supported them the best he could. Now he looked worn out, like a man ten years older than he really was.

But Ma was worn out too. She'd spent her life doing for everybody else, neglecting her own needs and appearance. And while the house was clean and neat, everything she owned was worn and shabby, from her faded flower-garden apron to the threadbare horsehair sofa in the living room.

She wore her salt-and-pepper hair short and straight. When I suggested she'd look great with a perm, she said, "I never could abide the smell." Then she had sighed and looked away, and I knew that was an excuse. Yet I knew her pride wouldn't let me pay.

"Why don't you take her to have it done as a birthday gift?"

Chapter Twenty-three

Dotty had suggested once.

It seemed a great idea at the time, but when her birthday came around, Jake decided she should have a new dress instead, and I was glad. The soft blue shirtwaist was the nicest thing she owned. Later, when she took off her apron to join the family at the table, I saw that she was wearing it today.

Anne Marie and Amy helped me set the table, after Amy peeked into the cake saver and squealed over her birthday cake. "Ooh, chocolate! I can't wait. Thank you, Aunt Celia." She hugged me fiercely, and I marveled at what a beautiful young lady she'd turned out to be.

"Did you tell Aunt Celia that you're graduating in February?" Ma Freeman's voice echoed pride in her youngest daughter.

Before Amy could reply, the screen door slammed, and the house was filled with noisy, enthusiastic greetings from the rest of the clan.

Sara June glowed as she reintroduced her husband. We'd been to their wedding last April. Jake grinned and kissed her on the cheek. "Nine months! You're an old married lady now," he said, grinning even wider when she blushed.

John had picked up Brian, who wrestled a war surplus Navy bag through the kitchen and onto the back porch. It was crammed with what must have been a month's worth of laundry. "This little jerk can't even keep himself in clean underwear." John laughed and ruffled his brother's thick black hair affectionately.

"Hey, man, give off, you'll ruin the wave." Brian smoothed back the lock that had escaped down his forehead, kissed his mother soundly and handed her a small box of Duz. "Here, Ma. Don't say I never brought you nothing."

Ma Freeman fairly beamed with pleasure. She accepted his kiss, then turned him toward the bathroom and popped his bottom like she had when he was six. "Go wash! Your hands are filthy!

"Heavenly days, you two, it's almost time for supper." She glowered at the kitchen door, where Dave and Pa Freeman had appeared, identical figures clad in blue jeans and T-shirts smeared with a thick layer of black grease.

Pa wore the same grass-stained jeans and a thin white shirt every weekday. Anne confided that he only showered and changed to slacks and a jacket for church on Sunday mornings.

Dave frowned, but his pa just chuckled and laid a meaty hand on the shoulder of his wife's dress. "Now, Mother," he said, "we had to get that engine running. Can't give the kid a broke-down car for his birthday, can we?"

But he already had. I wanted to grab a rag and wipe the greasy handprint from Ma's dress, then smack Dave's bottom just to get a reaction. He never said boo to his mother or the rest of us. Now he just ambled over to the kitchen sink, ran some water on his hands and slouched down in his place at the table.

"Did you get it running?" Jake broke the awkward silence, but I could see the gleam of anger in his eyes when his brother wouldn't look at him.

Dave shrugged. "It'll turn over. Needs a valve job, though."

Jake massaged his left shoulder with his right hand, a gesture left over from the years it had taken the muscles to heal. It rarely bothered him unless we had rain, but he'd continued to rub it out of habit when making a decision. "Bring it in on Monday, and I'll take a look."

It was an invitation sincerely made, but Dave just shrugged again and glowered at his plate. Jake ignored him. "Okay, Ma, we're hungry as a pack of wolves," he drawled. "Bring on the grub."

Everyone laughed, including Ma, and the noise resumed with four or five conversations going on at once. Ma took a bite of food now and then, but mostly she just looked around the table at her family, pride and contentment reflected in her eyes.

I noticed a hint of something else, though, when she looked at Dave. Worry? Fear? If he were mine, I'm sure I'd have felt some of both. He'd been such a compliant child. Friendly and outgoing. Until his sophomore year at high school, when he'd started hanging out with a rougher crowd. His grades had gone downhill, and his manners with them. Jake had tried to talk to him several times, but he'd only grown more sullen. It was a miracle he was still in school, and I wondered if Amy's success with an early graduation would help or hinder the situation.

No one even mentioned Tim. It was an unspoken rule that everyone adhered to whenever Ma was around. Privately we were concerned that she'd never dealt with his death. Certainly she'd grieved—we all had—but after a short time of mourning she'd locked it all away and refused to talk about her second son. It was as if he'd never been born.

After the dishes were done, Libby flitted from the garage, where the men had gathered around Dave's old/new hot rod, to the living room. She was obviously torn between her attraction to her Uncle Davy and the newly developed fondness for her Aunt Anne. While she was in the house, she practically draped herself over Anne's shoulder, drinking in every word. It became difficult to have an adult conversation.

I almost sent her away more than once. But Anne Marie seemed to enjoy her company, and Grandma Freeman declared herself "blessed by the presence of my angel." Libby grinned and I rolled my eyes at that pronouncement. But her doting relatives won, and I let her stay.

Chapter
Twenty-four

By the time we cut the cake and the twins opened presents, it was seven o'clock. The boys left moaning that they were "stuffed to the gills," but both were loaded down with enough leftovers to feed an army for a week.

Ma kissed Brian on the cheek. "Your pa will bring the laundry by tomorrow afternoon." She hugged John and scolded, "Drive carefully."

"That rear tire looks low to me, son," Pa Freeman commented. "Better get some air."

"Sure, Pa."

Sara June waved and blew kisses as she and Steven pulled out right behind the boys.

Ma dragged Amy off to the kitchen to help with dishes. "You all sit," she instructed. "We'll be done in a jiffy."

Libby sat on her knees by the coffee table, drawing in a new pencil book her grandparents had given her "so she won't be jealous of the twins." I had started to say, "She's much too old for that anymore." But Libby was delighted with the gift. Like I told Jake later, "It pleases your parents so to give her things, I guess we shouldn't ruin their fun."

Anne Marie leaned her head back against the sofa and closed

her eyes. I could read how tired she was in her pale skin and fading smile.

"Why don't you go on up to bed?" I spoke gently so as not to startle her. I remembered Mama's headaches and Aunt Rose's too. They had both suffered terribly for a time. Maybe Anne Marie had the same malady.

"What? And miss the chance to visit with you? I'm fine." She smiled at Jake and caressed my cheek. "But you're a dear to think of me."

"How are you, Anne, really?" Jake's tone was serious.

"I really am fine!" She sat up straighter and looked from us to the kitchen door and back again. "You don't have to worry about me. I'm not like Ma. I let myself grieve. Frank is gone. There's nothing I can do about that. I miss him terribly, but I know God has plans for me, or he wouldn't have left me behind." She sighed. "I just wish I knew what they were."

She looked at Jake. "I love Ma and Pa," she said earnestly. "You know I do, but . . ."

"But they're driving you crazy," Jake said.

Anne grinned. "How'd you guess?"

Jake smiled back at her. "They'd have me bonkers in a week. So why don't you find a roommate, move out on your own? Aren't you supposed to start work at St. Luke's in a week or so?"

Anne shifted her gaze to Libby, who held her pencil poised above the paper, intent on finding just the right angle for the eyebrows on a portrait she was sketching. I'd watched her erase it three times in the last ten minutes.

"I thought so," Anne replied absently, "but now I'm not so sure."

I started to ask why, but she interrupted, turning the conversation to Chuck, the extent of his injuries, his upcoming release from the hospital and his refusal to go back home.

The last time Jake and I had visited, we'd found him sitting in a chair beside his bed. His arms had been propped up on pillows, and he was exercising his fingers by trying to rub the scratches out of his leather jacket.

"This is trashed." He gave up and tossed it on the ground.

Dr. Fob walked into the room in time to hear the disgust in Chuck's voice. "Be thankful you were wearing it. It saved the hide on your back and chest." He nodded to Jake and me, then put one hand lightly on Chuck's shoulder and studied the chart. "Well, young man, do you think you can get along without us?"

Chuck's face was a study of surprise and fear. "You're booting me out?"

The doctor smiled. "I don't see why not. For the most part you're healing fine, and there doesn't seem to be any more swelling in the brain."

Chuck looked away toward the window. When he turned back, his face was empty of emotion. Dr. Fob didn't seem to notice.

"The casts can come off tomorrow. If everything looks okay, you can go home by the first of the week. Your father has made arrangements for physical therapy at Doctor's Hospital in San Diego. They have a fine facility. I'm sure you'll be in good hands."

"No."

"Excuse me?"

Chuck looked sullen again and carefully avoided our eyes. "I'm not going back there."

I took a breath and felt Jake squeeze my hand, telling me to keep still. We'd already discussed the possibility of Chuck's coming to live with us, but decided it was out of the question. Or rather, *Jake* decided, but his objections made sense. "We only have two bedrooms," he had pointed out, "and Libby is at the wrong age to bring that kind of trouble into the house." It hurt, but I had to admit he was right. Chuck still had a chip on his shoulder, "more like a two-by-four," as Jake said. I'd had to agree it would be an uncomfortable situation for all of us.

"But son . . ." The doctor had set his chart aside and was sitting on the edge of the bed, where Chuck had no choice but to look at him. "You have to understand that you'll need help for a while. It will be some time before you can walk on your own."

He held up his hand to stop Chuck's protest. "Hear me out." His voice toughened, and I thought that he must have a son of his own. "You are making progress, but the bones and muscles in your arms and legs are very tender and weak. In some cases your muscles have atrophied. The chances of a fall and reinjury are high. You've come too far to let that happen. You need someone to help you get around, transportation to and from therapy . . ."

He let the sentence hang and slapped Chuck lightly on the knee. "You're not a child. Think about it, and if you come up with any other options let me know."

Dr. Fob flashed Jake and me a look that said, *Talk some sense into him,* then turned and left the room. "I'll see you tomorrow," he called over his shoulder and was gone.

"I can't accept their terms." Chuck kept his head turned, eyes fixed on the window. I thought maybe he would fling himself at the glass.

Like Jimmy Wilson's bird. I shivered at the memory.

I was nine and Chuckie three when a neighbor boy, Jimmy Wilson, found the bird. Its feet had frozen to Mrs. Wilson's wire clothesline. "Just a dirty ol' starling," Mrs. Wilson had declared. "Best leave it alone and let nature have its way." But Jimmy couldn't leave it, especially not when Chuckie saw it and set up a wail they must have heard clear into town. "Shut him up, Cissy," Jimmy had hollered over the noise, "and go heat some water. I'll get a shoebox and meet you back here."

We lined the box with a scrap of blanket from Mrs. Wilson's ragbag, then I held the starling, its bird heart whirring like a wound-up top, while Jimmy slowly poured the lukewarm water over both of its feet. It's a good thing I was holding it, because the poor thing fainted dead away.

At first we thought it was dead. I laid it gently in the make-shift bed and took it in by Mama's stove. In a few hours it had recovered enough to stand. It was still too weak to fly, so Jimmy dug an old birdcage out of the attic and lined it with the front page of the *Pike Review*.

The bird perched still as stone for three days. Then one morning it spread its wings and flew into the side of the cage. Jimmy said it didn't make a sound, just flung itself against the wires like a soul possessed. By the time he got it outside to turn it loose, the starling had collapsed, exhausted and bleeding, on the bottom of the cage. It died an hour later.

Chuckie had cried for days.

Jake and I had left Chuck's room that day so Aunt Rose and Uncle Edward could go in. The staff had let us break the rules once for our family meeting, but they made it clear we weren't to make it a habit. "The rule is two visitors at a time." The floor nurse had been kind but firm.

"When they came back out," I told Anne now, "I asked Aunt Rose if Chuck had made a decision. 'Why, of course, dear,' she said, 'he's coming home with us.' I swear, Anne, she didn't even blink an eye, did she, Jake?"

Anne laughed. "I guess, after all you've told me, that would be the natural thing. Still"—she looked thoughtful—"your aunt will have her hands full with both your uncle and brother to care for. I wonder if they really understand what's involved."

"Does that mean I can't visit Nana Rose and Grandpa Edward anymore?" Libby's voice trembled, and her fist was closed so tight around her pencil I thought she'd snap it in two.

I looked at Jake. His wrinkled forehead showed me he was puzzled by her question too. "Of course not, Libby." I tried to smile. "Whatever gave you that idea?"

"Daddy?" Her eyes welled up, and she ran to stand beside his chair. "Aunt M said I'm not supposed to be around that creep. How can I visit Grandpa Ed if he's living there?"

I thought Jake would break the arms on his mother's cane-back chair. He was gripping them so tightly his knuckles had turned white, and his face was a ghastly shade of purple.

"Jake," I warned. Then I held out my arms. "Come here, Libby," I said. "We need to talk."

Jake's look said plainly, *So do we.*

Chapter
Twenty-five

I pacified Libby with the promise of a visit to Aunt Rose's next Sunday afternoon. Chuck would be there, hopefully settled in by then. In the meantime we would have to try to neutralize some of Mary Margaret's poison.

Jake looked grim, both hands closed around the steering wheel, concentrating harder than he needed to on the road ahead. I slid over and began to rub the rigid muscles in his neck and shoulder.

"It's partly our fault, you know." His eyes narrowed, and I hurried on before he could get started again. "Well, it is, darling. We should have explained the situation to Libby. She's not a baby anymore. We could have told her Chuck wanted to meet her but the hospital said no visitors under sixteen. It would have been the truth, and maybe Mary Margaret's tirades wouldn't have had so much effect."

Jake's voice was calm, and I knew he was holding himself under tight control. "I told you weeks ago we shouldn't let your cousin have Libby so often. She takes her places she has no business going yet."

"Last week they went to Disneyland!"

"Right. And the week before that a drive-in movie, and the

week before that it was cruising Hollywood Boulevard with her latest boyfriend. Of all her harebrained ideas, that one takes the cake!"

His voice had risen in pitch with the last sentence. I cringed and looked over my shoulder. Libby slept peacefully, stretched across the back seat, her feet propped up on the armrest.

"Next thing you know, it'll be a bar." He took a breath and looked me in the eye. "Well, there won't be a next time. I forbid it, Celia, do you understand? Mary Margaret is not to see Libby unless one of us is there."

I thought he was blowing the whole thing out of proportion, but I decided it was best not to say anything right then.

* * *

Anne had been right; Aunt Rose did have her hands full. Too full, I told Jake later. We all agreed she would need some help, but by the time we left on Sunday evening, nothing had been decided.

The meeting between Libby and Chuck went well, I thought. She was shy at first, but when he nodded toward the empty space on the sofa beside him and offered her the funnies, she accepted with a smile.

He looked exhausted. Aunt Rose confided that the week had been one ordeal after another, from finding a comfortable position for the bed in Billy's room to Chuck's first attempt at therapy. He'd been in so much pain by the time they returned, it had taken Aunt Rose and Uncle Edward's strength combined to help him up the stairs.

"He refuses to sleep downstairs," Aunt Rose said. "I don't know what I'd have done if your uncle hadn't been there."

Uncle Edward was still an invalid himself. He was up now most of the day and could walk alone as long as he used a cane. But he tired easily and couldn't sit or stand in one position for very long. He was in no condition to help Aunt Rose haul

Chuck up and down the stairs.

* * *

Dotty called the next day to remind me the girls had choir practice after school for the Christmas concert. "They have to try on their robes and the whole bit. Why don't you let Libby come here for dinner, and we'll bring her home later?"

"Oh, Dotty, thank you. I'd forgotten all about it." I realized that I'd forgotten about several things lately: cookies for Libby's class party and a promise to work in the nursery at church last Sunday. Dotty had come through each time.

"It's okay, Celia, you've had other things on your mind. How is your brother, by the way?"

"He's better, but it's too big a load for Aunt Rose. I wish we lived closer so I could be more help to her."

"Why doesn't she just hire a nurse?"

I paused. To me the reasons were obvious: they couldn't afford it, and neither could we. The accident had drained what little savings they had, and Jake had mortgaged everything we owned for his auto shop. That was a sore point for me, yet I knew I wasn't being fair. Jake's dreams were important, and he supported us well. Still, with the cost of living and Libby's school, there just wasn't anything left over.

"Celia?"

I realized Dotty was waiting for an answer. "Thanks, Dotty, I'll talk to her."

"If we can help, I could talk to Sam . . ."

"Oh, Dot, you're the best, but we couldn't let you do that. You do enough as it is." I quickly changed the subject. "We'll pick Libby up after dinner so you don't have to go out."

When we hung up, I felt tired, like someone had pulled a plug and drained the joy out of the day. I decided to take a walk, thinking that maybe some fresh air would help. But when I opened the front door, cold gray drops of rain blew into the screen. I closed it again and forced myself to tackle the hall closet. It had needed cleaning for weeks.

As I sorted colored thread and refolded a stack of linen napkins I hadn't used in years, I thought about the stack of paperwork waiting for me at the office. I was scheduled to go in tomorrow, and the prospect lifted my spirits. They were always glad to see me. "You're a lifesaver," Mr. Johnson had said last week. "I don't know how we ever got along without you."

Jake had gotten used to me working, and I was careful not to let my hours interfere with family time. He had wondered, though, why I didn't find a job that actually paid something for my time.

"Because," I reminded him, "then I couldn't set my own hours. Besides, I like this job, and you agreed it was a worthwhile cause."

He couldn't argue with that.

* * *

The school concert went well. The children knew the words to every song, and no one missed a note. Libby's choir was the best, of course. Mrs. Reynolds, the music teacher, had handpicked students from the upper three grades. Libby and Rachel shared the last two spaces in the first row. Dotty and I smiled and clapped. I'd had to drag Jake to the event, and Sam came in late, but when they saw the girls, their faces beamed and they applauded as loud as anyone.

Toward the end Jake grew restless, and I felt myself getting fidgety. I was relieved when we were asked to stand and join the choirs in singing "Silent Night." The words of all the verses came easily to my lips, but I was dismayed to find that for some reason they didn't seem to reach my heart.

In the days that followed I tried hard to catch the Christmas spirit. But as I wrapped up Libby's shoe skates, a new watch for Jake and a shirt that Chuck would most likely never wear,

I found myself sinking deeper into a state of gloom.

I told myself I was being ridiculous. God had given me so much, but all I could do was mope.

I tried counting my blessings. Uncle Edward and Chuck were both alive and healing. We had good food, nice clothing, a comfortable home, a warm and loving family. Yet I felt there was something missing, something I was searching for but hadn't found.

True, Grace still hadn't come around. She refused to even meet us or, worse, visit Chuck. His parents had washed their hands of him. He wanted no contact with them either, and Aunt Rose had said to let it be. "He'll come around in time, Cissy. So will they. Our job is to love them, help Charles get well and, of course, pray."

I willed myself to pack away my gloom with the leftover ribbons and bows. We had finally convinced Aunt Rose that she couldn't do Christmas all herself this year.

"Oh, we're still going over there," I told Dotty when she invited us to spend the day with them. "But we've made her swear not to do a thing. Mary Margaret's going over early to help her clean and decorate, and I'm bringing most of the food. The pies are in the oven right now. I thought I'd cook the turkey a day ahead, slice it and save it in the juice. It won't be quite the same, but for this year it will have to do."

"Mary Margaret's going over?"

"I know, I couldn't believe it either. I tried to tell her that with Libby out of school, I could come and it really would be easier to do the turkey over there. She wouldn't listen. She says it's her responsibility. You know how stubborn she can be when she gets a bug in her bonnet."

"Oh my," Dotty chuckled. "What a bee's nest that will be."

I tried to be positive. "Maybe not. She's promised to behave. She may not agree with her parents' decision, but they made it clear to her that Chuck is there for the duration. Surely she's grown up enough to honor that."

Dotty sighed. "I hope you're right, Celia girl, I really do." She changed the subject. "Have a merry Christmas, darling, and give my love to Jake. We'll see you at our house New Year's Eve."

Chapter
Twenty-six

"**Mary Margaret** has me stymied," I admitted to Jake. "Did you see how solicitous she was this weekend? She went out of her way to be nice to Chuck, even though I know it galled her to do it. And he was so sullen! You'd have thought she was a saint and he some poor lost waif she'd been called to save."

Jake chuckled and backed the car into the garage. "I know. It was sickening. I'd almost rather see her be a snob. And it only made your brother worse. I swear I saw him raise his crutch at least three times and then back off. It would have made his day to clobber her."

"Jake!" I looked pointedly toward the back seat, but Libby only yawned and stretched. As soon as the car came to a stop, she ran into the house to check on her goldfish. She was back in under thirty seconds with the report that Lucy and Desi had at least a dozen babies swimming with them in the tank.

"Oh dear, we'll have to put them in a different bowl. Go feed them, and I'll be right there."

Jake opened the trunk and handed me an armload of opened presents. Libby had adored her shoe skates. She'd been asking for a pair since they started offering lessons at the Shamrock Roller Rink. She and Rachel practically lived there on Saturdays, and they'd gone three times the first week of Christmas vacation.

I picked up the Nancy Drew mysteries she'd hardly looked at. She'd enjoyed them so much the year before that I'd told Aunt Rose to get her two more. This year she'd said a polite thank-you, but she'd put them back in the box and hadn't looked at them since. Now I discovered two of Mary Margaret's true-crime books in the bottom of the box. I put them back and headed for the house before Jake could see.

"Mother!" Libby's screams almost made me drop my armload on the floor.

I dumped everything on the couch and rushed into her room. She stood pointing to the tank, a look of horror on her face. "Do something!" she wailed. "You have to do something. There's only six babies left and I think . . ." She buried her face in her hands. "I think Lucy and Desi are eating them!"

Jake ran panting into the room. "What is going on in here? All that screeching, I thought someone was dead!"

"They are, Daddy, they are!" Libby's sobs grew louder, and she began to stomp her feet on the hardwood floor. "Lucy and Desi are cannibals. They're eating their babies!"

"Oh, for . . . Celia, go get a bowl or something, and I'll try to fish them out of there."

"I think it's too late," I said and tried to put my arms around my sobbing daughter. Libby pushed me away and ran to the tank. The water was clouded by bits of debris, but the two adult goldfish swam alone.

* * *

"I wasn't trying for your uncle," Chuck said out of the blue.

He's your uncle too, I wanted to remind him, but I kept still and waited for him to go on.

He studied the cheap platinum ring on his finger. He'd forced it on as soon as the swelling had gone down enough.

"Some chick in pedal pushers and a halter top was hitchhiking on the other side of the road," he continued. "I thought, why not go out happy? So I swerved over to the other lane, and next thing I know, splat. I'm dog meat."

I had to bite my tongue to keep from scolding him about his language. Mama was probably turning over in her grave. "Oh Chuck," I said, "why?"

He cocked his head and for an instant flashed that little boy smile. "If you can't guess that one, sis, I'm not the one to tell you."

I felt my face go red. It was easier to be with him when he was sulking and quiet than to carry on a conversation, especially one that touched on his problems. I wanted to run out of the room, go home to my family and bake pumpkin bread for New Year's Eve. "Charles Summers, you know that's not what I meant."

He smiled again, a fake smile this time, but had the grace to lower his eyes.

I decided to change the subject. "In the notebook you said you left home, but you didn't say where you went. Surely you had some kind of life during those six years—a job . . ." I started to ask about a sweetheart, but in light of his crude remark about the girl on the highway I decided to let it be.

He shrugged. "Yeah, some kind of life. But you don't want to hear about that." He looked down at the ring that now slid up and down his finger like it was two sizes too big. "I had a job, slinging hash at Stobbie's Bar and Grill. Had a girl too. Then Korea, then BANG." He pointed his finger at the wall and pretended to pull a trigger. "No more girl, and scrambled eggs instead of brains."

I looked at this young man who was my brother and saw nothing in his face that I could recognize except for the crooked grin that flashed true now and then. The damp blond curls were coming back in straight and dry as straw. Even his eyes were different—still blue, but darker, like ink spilled in a clear, deep pool.

I didn't understand, and he knew it. Just for a moment his face softened, and he touched my hand. "It's okay, sis. Maybe someday . . ." He let the sentence hang and closed his eyes. "Why don't you go now? Go on home to Jake and Libby. They need you more than I do." He smiled and rubbed one hand across his sunken stomach. "I have Rose."

I kissed his cheek and left him sitting in an easy chair next to Billy's window.

Aunt Rose must have been waiting in the hall. She hurried by me with a tray piled high with sandwiches and chips, a glass of water and an assortment of pills. "I'll be down in a minute, dear. Would you please check on your uncle for me? He's on the patio, of all things. I told him he'd freeze to death, but you know how stubborn he is."

Aunt Rose looked like she'd aged ten years in the last six months. Her hair had turned a solid gray, like Mama's just before she died. It would have been pretty if only she had time to fix it. It had been over a year since she'd had a perm, and I made a mental note to pick up one of those new Toni home permanents I'd seen at Woolworth's and surprise her. Maybe Dotty would come along and do it while I helped with Chuck and Uncle Edward. Jake and Sam could watch the kids.

I shook my head at my mental rambling. I'd been doing that a lot lately, making up scenes in my head like I was writing a play. Mary Margaret said it was because I was unhappy with my real life and had to conjure up sweetness and light. Or else go insane. She didn't say *like your mother,* but I knew that was what she meant, and it hurt.

It scared me too, a little. I couldn't help but remember how Mama had gone off into her own head when life got hard, a make-believe world where she and Papa lived a happy life with all their children by their side. There were times, though, when she faced reality. Those were painful times, when she recognized the truth and recorded it in letters.

The letters! I stopped dead on the stairs. I'd thought about Mama's letters when we first learned that "John" was Chuck, but I hadn't thought of them since—at least not at a time when I could do something about it. They were in my dresser, in a shoebox in the bottom drawer.

Mostly they had been written for Papa. Rambling pages on which she poured out her feelings, hurts and frustrations. Guilty letters filled with accusations, apologies, vows of forgiveness. Things that must have been as difficult to write as they were for me to read.

I'd skipped over some; they were private, after all. Some things a daughter doesn't need to know. But there were several addressed to me. And one each to all the others: Krista, Chuck and Baby Grace. Even one to the other baby, the one buried out on Harris Hill back in Pike.

I wondered if I should give Chuck his now. And if not now, when?

Chapter
Twenty-seven

Anne Marie called Aunt Rose on the first day of 1956. By January 3 she was installed, lock, stock and baggage, in Mary Margaret's old room.

"She wasn't happy with what they offered her at St. Luke's," I explained to Jake that night at supper. "She told Aunt Rose she'd felt a burden to help out ever since she heard about the situation with Chuck. When the hospital offered her only half of what she was making in San Francisco, I guess that just confirmed it."

Jake raised his eyebrows, but a little smile tugged at the corner of his mouth. "So my sister has moved in with Rose and Ed to nurse poor Chuckie back to health." He didn't even try to keep the sarcasm out of his voice.

I wanted to flip his lip, like Mama used to do when Krista or I sassed her. "At least she has some compassion," I said, unable to keep the hurt out of my voice, but Jake didn't seem to notice.

"Well," he conceded, "I guess it's one solution. She told me at Christmas she can live on Frank's life insurance for a while yet. This way Rose gets some help with the invalids, Anne gets out from under Ma's thumb, and"—he swatted my backside as I turned to set the plates on the counter—"you get to stay home where you belong."

* * *

Work at Children's Charities had slowed to a trickle. The old Quonset hut we used for an office had been condemned, and someone had carted it off around the middle of January. It would be at least two months before we could open for business in another building.

Mr. Johnson and some of the other board members had taken work home. I had brought some typing home too, but the work seemed boring with no one around to talk to.

"When we get back to normal," Mr. Johnson had said, "we may ask you to help review some of the children's cases for placement. It would mean more hours, but maybe we could sweeten the pot with a small paycheck." He smiled and squeezed my shoulder. "Just think about it. We'll talk more later."

I hadn't told Jake yet, or Dotty either, but I knew if the chance came along, I'd grab it in a minute.

* * *

"I have to get out of here," I told Dotty one morning in early March. "Let's go to the park—just the two of us, like we used to before we were married."

"Good grief, Celia, I can't remember that far back. Besides, I have six loads of wash, and I promised the twins we'd bake cookies this afternoon."

"Come on, Dot." I couldn't believe the whine in my voice, but the feeling of euphoria when I thought about a day at the park was more than I could resist. "You know Jake would be furious if I went alone. Please say you'll come. I'll pack some sandwiches and pick you up in an hour. We can buy snow cones and ride the merry-go-round."

"Celia Freeman, what's got into you?"

"One hour," I said and hung up before she could say no. My heart was pounding like I'd just won a race, and I felt younger than I'd felt in ages, younger than Libby or Rachel, irresponsible, and . . .

"Free," I said aloud. Free and more excited than I'd felt in years.

*   *   *

"Okay, Cissy, this had better be good." Dotty slid into the Chevy and threw her sweater on the back seat. She had on a shirtwaist dress and penny loafers without the pennies. And, I thought, a gleam in her eye that matched my own.

I tugged on the strap to my canary-yellow sundress. I'd bought it last spring on sale at the May Company and worn it only once.

"Wow, you look nice. But aren't you freezing?"

"Yes, but I don't need a mother, Dotty. At least not today." I pulled carefully onto the new freeway that ran from Valley Boulevard all the way into Los Angeles and Garfield Park. It cut at least thirty minutes off the trip.

I glanced at my friend. She had her head back on the seat, eyes closed, letting the breeze from the open window tangle her hair. There was a contented smile on her face I hadn't seen in a while.

I stayed in the righthand lane and, in spite of the urge to hurry, concentrated on keeping my speed at forty-five. Jake would be upset enough if he knew I was out gallivanting on a Wednesday morning. He'd be livid if I came home with a ticket.

I took the Griffith Boulevard exit and followed the rolling pavement past acres of grass and trees to the hub of the park. There were few cars in the lot this time of day. A mother with a toddler and a baby in a stroller walked slowly toward the entrance to the zoo. A couple in their early twenties moved hand in hand across the grass and spread a blanket under the protective cover of a willow tree. A few children soared on swings and hung from monkey bars while their guardians dozed on wooden benches set around the parameter of the play yard.

I grabbed Dotty's hand and dragged her toward the merry-go-round. It was almost noon, and the sign said OPEN AT 2:00 P.M. Scurrying on, we ignored the tuna sandwiches in my basket and bought hot dogs from a vendor cart. For a moment I wished it were Jake with me instead of Dot. But I knew that was a foolish wish; Jake was far too busy to come to the park. Especially on a weekday. Anyway, I could just hear him say, "Why would I want to go to the park? Besides, the Giants are playing Los Angeles. Live!"

We washed the hot dogs down with Coke, grabbed our sweaters and walked to the lake. Dotty broke off pieces of leftover bun and threw them to the ducks. They squabbled over the crumbs like a bunch of naughty children, then trailed after us, squawking greedily for more.

The noisy entourage finally gave up and retreated into the chilly water. Dotty and I lit on a bench and stuck our bare legs out in front of us to catch some warmth from the sun. I closed my eyes and listened. Except for bird song and an occasional animal cry from the zoo, the park was quiet.

I found my thoughts drifting here and there, like cloud pictures changing with the wind: Jake and I in a row boat on Bear Lake, Krista sipping tea with her Samantha doll, Mama singing lullabies to Baby Grace, the ballerina on Libby's music box twirling and twirling while the tinny notes tinkled slower and slower as it wound down.

"Listen, Celia, the merry-go-round is open now. Do you still want to ride?"

Dotty's voice brought me back to the present with a start.

For a moment I felt hollow, empty, reluctant to leave my dreams.

"What's wrong, girl?" Dotty took my hand and pressed a peppermint into my palm. "Eat this," she said, "you look pale. Now tell me what this is all about."

"Oh, Dotty, I don't know. It's hard to put it into words. I feel so restless lately. And alone. Libby has her friends, and Jake is busy with the shop. Even Aunt Rose doesn't need me any longer now that Anne Marie is there."

Dotty nodded. "It's too bad you and Jake only have one child. I never have time to feel lonely."

"No thank you! No offense, but Libby is a handful. I don't need more children to contend with." I was surprised by my own words, but realized they were true. I'd quit dreaming of another child some time ago.

"A job, then. A full-time one with pay. You're a great typist. A good secretary, too. Some poor overworked executive would hire you in a minute."

"Full time? Jake would have my hide. You know he'd never hear of it. Who would cook his dinners and wash his socks? Who would drive Libby to piano lessons?" I took a breath and shook my head in disbelief. "Would you listen to me?" I stood in frustration and headed off across the grass.

Dotty fell into step beside me, her face a study of curiosity and something else. Fear? Was I scaring her? Did she think I was losing it, like Mama? The thought had been in the back of my own mind these past few months. I shook it off. It was too horrible to contemplate.

I stopped and turned to face her. "I'm fine, Dot, I really am. I certainly don't need more to do." I sighed and sank down on the grass, grateful for the full-gored skirt that covered my legs and the tree-branch shadows that hid my reddened face.

"I know part of it is Chuck. The disappointment of who he

really is. It's like finding my brother and losing him again." I plucked a handful of grass and tossed it into the wind.

"And Grace. Or Florence. Whoever she is. How can she treat us this way? Her own kin! Chuck loves her, Dotty, he really does, and she won't even acknowledge he exists." I realized my voice was growing louder and higher in pitch, but I couldn't stop the venom that seemed to spill from some unknown part of me. A part I had no control of whatsoever.

"I've written her three times, Dotty. But do you think Miss-High-and-Mighty would answer even once? She won't return Aunt Rose's phone calls either. She's positively rude."

Dotty stayed quiet, and I fished a tissue out of my skirt pocket.

"Maybe you should just stop." Dotty's voice was quiet, but it held a hint of impatience.

"Stop what?"

"Stop trying to change them." She looked straight into my eyes and didn't blink. "You can't, you know. Maybe you should just let Chuck and Grace deal with their own lives, and get your own back in order."

"Dotty Levi!" But the love on her face melted my protests. I knew she was telling me the truth. I'd been stewing in my own self-pity, trying to fix everybody else's lives and mad because they didn't thank me for it.

I lowered my eyes as she put a protective arm around my shoulder. "Look, girl, it'll all work out, you'll see." She looked at her watch. "Now, we'd better scoot. There's a storm brewing, and the kids will wonder where we are."

I nodded and pushed my arms into my sweater. The wind had picked up, blowing in from the north, twirling scraps of paper and forming tiny whitecaps on the lake. The ducks had drifted to the shelter of an oak tree by the bank, heads tucked neatly under downy wings.

By the time we picked the children up at school, the rain had soaked the pavement and overflowed the curbs. Libby and I ran from the driveway to the house, ducking hailstones the size of dimes.

Chapter
Twenty-eight

Chuck seemed to be healing faster under Anne's ministrations. His attitude had improved some too. I noticed he smiled more often and called Aunt Rose "Rosebud," a nickname he'd picked up from Jake.

Still, he wouldn't confide in anyone. He talked to me about Mama and Papa and things that happened in the past. He seemed interested in my stories about St. Stephen's and growing up at Uncle Edward's. He and Jake talked politics, baseball and current events, surprising me by agreeing on almost everything.

Libby was his special favorite. They spent hours reading together—everything from comic books to Bible stories. Libby knew the latter all by heart. But she delighted in reading them to Chuck, and he listened intently—sometimes with a frown, sometimes with a wistful smile.

"Uncle Chuck likes the story of the prodigal son best," she confided one Sunday evening during the drive home from Uncle Edward's.

Jake looked at me in surprise.

"What makes you say that, sweetheart?" I asked.

She leaned over the front seat. "Because he asks me to read

it to him every time. I finally told him where to look it up so he could read it for himself when I'm not there."

Out of the mouths of babes, I thought. "I'm sure he appreciates that," I said, patting her hand.

She nodded solemnly. "He said he knew it once. He just forgot. Uncle Chuck went to Sunday school too, you know, when he was little, but he quit going when he got older." She paused. "He made me promise to never quit. And I won't, Mom." She crossed her heart. "I made a solemn vow."

I poked Jake in the leg, and he covered his laugh by tuning in a ball game on the radio.

* * *

I knew I had to resolve the conflict with Mary Margaret sooner or later, but I hated confrontations, especially with someone as stubborn and vulnerable as my cousin.

"How can I tell her she can't see Libby because she's a bad influence?" I asked Dotty. "She already thinks all Christians are stuck-up snobs; I don't want to alienate her altogether."

"Try to say something positive first. She must have some strong points."

"She loves Libby, that's for sure. And us too, in her own way. She's been wonderful company for Chuck. She goes out there every Saturday so Anne can have the day off. Aunt Rose says they play chess and backgammon and talk for hours. M told her mother that she and Chuck speak the same language, whatever that means."

"But I thought she hated his guts!"

I shook my head. "I'm not sure what happened. The only thing I can figure out is that she got to know him better over Christmas. Then when Anne showed up, M seemed insulted that her mother would need someone else to help out."

"Is she jealous? She has to work, for goodness sake. Is her mother supposed to just make do until the weekend?"

A Time to Search

"I don't know what she's thinking; I never do. In any case, she spends as much time over there now as possible. She hasn't asked for Libby in three months. Not since she and that Elmo character broke up."

"The guy with the souped-up Ford? Well, you knew that wouldn't last. He was six years younger than she."

"Eight. And while we're on the subject, what am I going to do about Libby?"

Dotty sighed. "You'll just have to wait until she asks to take her somewhere and deal with it then. It's too bad Jake . . ."

"I know. He lays down edicts, then expects me to carry them out. But he's right. We can't let Libby run wild, even if she is with an adult."

"Well, I don't envy you, girl."

I heard familiar music coming down the street. "Uh-oh. I'll talk to you later. I have to catch the Helms truck—we're out of bread, and I don't have time to go to the store."

I bought a dozen doughnuts too, an after-school treat for Libby and her friends. She and Rachel had decided to play at our house today, and they were bringing a new girl who'd just moved to California from back East somewhere.

"She's lonely, Mom," Libby had told me that morning. "She doesn't have friends yet." It made me feel good to know the girls were sensitive to someone else's needs.

* * *

Mary Margaret called that night at seven-thirty. As luck would have it, Libby was at the dining-room table doing homework and grabbed the phone. She listened for a minute, then covered the mouthpiece with her hand.

"Mom!" she hollered loud enough to wake the dead.

"I'm right here, Libby, you don't have to shout."

"Sorry," she whispered. "It's Aunt M. She wants to know if I can go to the movies on Saturday."

Chapter Twenty-eight

I looked at Jake, who glared his answer from across the room.

"Let me talk to her, honey. Why don't you take your homework to your room? It's quieter there."

"But Mom—"

"No buts! Now scoot." I took the phone and patted her bottom for emphasis.

She moved a few feet, then turned around. "Mom, please!" Her face was red, and fat tears ran down her cheeks.

I put the receiver to my ear. "M? I'll have to call you back. Ten minutes, I promise." I hung up and turned to my suddenly distraught daughter. "Liberty Jane, what on earth has gotten into you?" I bent to pick up the book Libby had tossed on the floor.

"You never listen to me!" she wailed.

"Libby, don't raise your voice to your mother." Jake's voice could have announced the Second Coming.

"Daddy!" She stamped her foot in frustration. "I'm just trying to tell you that I don't want to go to the show on Saturday. Rachel and I have lessons at the Shamrock."

"Keep it up and you won't go anywhere, Miss Sass." Jake was breathing fire, and Libby matched him breath for breath.

"Mom!" She tossed her head and threw her notebook and pencil in the same direction as the book. "You won't let me say anything. I'm old enough to have a life!" She turned and stormed into her room. The bedsprings squeaked, and even after the door slammed tight, we could hear her ragged sobs.

Jake pushed up from the sofa, looking like the angel of death.

"Jake," I said.

Just as suddenly his shoulders drooped, and he sagged back down. When I moved toward the bedroom, he held his hand up. "Just leave it, Celia. At least until we all calm down."

I sighed and turned back to the telephone. Mary Margaret answered on the second ring. "I'm sorry, M. I know you're late for work. But I'm afraid Saturday's out. I don't think Libby will be going anywhere for a while."

* * *

"Where did we go wrong?" I asked Aunt Rose on Saturday morning.

Her laugh stung a little. "Don't fret so, Cissy. All girls go through that stage. Boys too, if I recall." She paused like she always did when we talked about Billy. I could almost see the faraway smile she wore when she remembered something he had said or done. "Of course they seem to grow up quicker these days. Have patience with her, dear. Things may get worse before they get better. Just remember, 'this too shall pass.' "

Aunt Rose's words of wisdom did little to soothe the tension between Jake and Libby. She acted the same as always toward me—well, maybe a little more aloof—but she gave him the cold shoulder and wouldn't talk to him for a week.

"She gets smart and starts a ruckus and it's suddenly my fault. Why, Celia? Just tell me why."

I shook my head. Truth to tell, I didn't know what to say. I didn't remember ever acting that way at Libby's age. Or later either. I had felt neglected at times, and angry when Papa came home drunk, but I never said a thing aloud. Not to him and Mama anyway. But we'd had so many problems then. No money, no food and a move to California from our home in Pike. I guess I didn't have time to "want a life," as Libby put it.

I could have reminded Jake about a certain young man who hid out in our car shed with a bottle of Papa's whiskey. He had wanted his own life too and thought the only way to find it was to get away from his ma and her list of chores. Of course he was older. And if he'd expressed himself to his folks the way Libby had, he'd have suffered a taste of his pa's razor strap.

I shuddered. We'd never had to spank Libby much, and I was glad. "A beating accomplishes naught, and it only makes the truant wary of getting caught." I'd read that somewhere and had to agree.

Still, we had to do something. After a week of no privileges, just dinner and homework after school, and no skating on Saturday, Libby simmered down and started being civil.

"They're growing up," Dotty admitted on the phone. "I found Rachel and that new girl, Carol, practicing dance steps in front of my full-length mirror. In their stocking feet, no less. I wondered why she had so many holes in her bobby socks lately."

"So that's it. Libby's are that way too. I can't begin to get the dirt out of them." I felt uneasy about the music she'd been listening to. The beat was fast and the words were garbled. The ones that made any sense had lyrics that would have made Grandma Eva blush.

"Do you think we should do something about it? I hate to take away her radio, but . . ."

"Celia, they're just dancing—and with each other, not with boys. Face it, girl, we can't keep them babies forever."

Chapter
Twenty-nine

I still hadn't said anything to Jake about going to the park. Dotty hadn't said anything either, and I was grateful. I wasn't sure he would understand my feelings. How could he if I didn't understand them myself? Besides, by June he was spending more and more time at the shop. He worked overtime at least twice a week and even some Saturday mornings.

"I thought you were going to hire someone to take over on Saturdays," I said as he folded the morning paper and headed for the door.

"Can't afford it yet." He dropped a kiss on my forehead right above my nose.

I frowned. "I thought you said things were going well."

"Not that well." He smiled and grabbed the car keys from the corner of the sink, where he had left them the night before. "Besides, if I do the work, it's more for us and for the vacation fund."

I'd been hearing about this vacation fund for months but had yet to see a penny of it or hear any specific plans.

"But we need you home more, Jake. I need you home." He was out the door before I got it halfway said.

It was Libby's first Saturday of freedom since her tantrum

the week before. She and Rachel had conned me into letting them walk to Carol's. Carol lived ten blocks west of Wells Street, which meant they had to cross Valley Boulevard, but I figured it was a good place to start if Libby wanted more independence.

I'd met Carol's mother at school. She was a quiet soul with a servant's heart and patience that put me to shame. We worked together on the seventh-grade end-of-school party, and she spent hours making decorations and telephoning for prize donations. The party was still a month away, but her job was done, and she had offered to help me round up refreshments as well.

I had just hung up the phone after talking another mother into baking three dozen peanut-butter cookies when all three girls bopped in, rolling their eyes and giggling behind their hands.

"Hold it, you three." I stepped into their path on the way to Libby's room. "What's so funny?" They had me giggling too, and I had just thought how nice it was to see them having fun when Libby spoke up.

"You really don't want to know, Mom." She stole a glance at Rachel and burst into new laughter.

Rachel assumed a sober air. "She's right, Aunt Celia, you would be embarrassed."

Carol snorted. "My mother wouldn't be embarrassed; she'd be mad as H-E double toothpicks."

Libby and Rachel stared at her in horror, then looked at me, presumably to see what I would do.

The world had changed since I was a child, and nothing had prepared me for it. Still, I made it clear that certain language was not allowed.

When they saw that I meant business, the girls told me that someone burned a dirty word into the Fergusons' lawn. "A really dirty word, Mom. I'm not going to say it."

"Me either!"

"It's the F word," Carol spouted, "and I bet I know who did it."

"The . . . ? Oh, my stars! Poor Mrs. Ferguson."

"They did it with kerosene. See, first you outline the word in chalk, then fill in the space with kerosene. It burns the grass away, and a few days later you can see the—" Carol quickly stopped when she caught the looks on all our faces, and she turned beet-red.

"I . . . I've never done it myself." Her eyes widened in panic. "You gotta believe me, Mrs. Freeman, I only know 'cause my brother told me how."

I said a prayer for wisdom and put my arm around the shaking girl. "I believe you, dear. Now go on, all of you, into the kitchen. There are cookies in the cookie jar and milk in the fridge."

Poor Mrs. Ferguson. It was a horrible prank. The problem was, the Fergusons thought more of their dichondra than they did other people, especially kids. They made no bones about screaming at the children to stay off the lawn. Mr. Ferguson could cuss like a drunken sailor and made no bones about that either. But except for run-ins with a parent or two, they stayed pretty much to themselves and didn't bother anyone.

They didn't help anyone either. Jake and I had avoided them since the incident with Jingles and the snake. The Swansons across the street had spread the word that they were Communists; true or not, the rumor stuck. All of the neighbors avoided them like the plague, and the Fergusons made it clear they liked it that way. I knew they wouldn't appreciate my interference now. Still, my conscience wouldn't let it be. I called Jake at the shop, but he wasn't very helpful.

"It's an old trick, Celia. Probably some boys from the neighborhood getting back at them."

"But darling, shouldn't we at least say something?"

"Like what, for crying out loud? If you want to knock on their door and tell them you're sorry, go ahead. But they'll just think we did it and call the cops, or sue us like they did before."

"Thank you, dear, for your understanding."

"Trust me, babe, the best thing to do is leave it alone. Look, I'm sorry, but the Harrisons' transmission is spread all over the floor. I have to get to it if I'm gonna make it home in time for dinner. We'll talk about this later, okay?"

Later, on the way to Sam and Dotty's, Jake conceded that destroying the Fergusons' lawn was a dirty prank. "I'm sure they reported it. But if you see any young punks hanging around, let me know and we'll call the police."

* * *

"Celia, come sit. It's your deal." Jake helped himself to another chocolate-chip cookie from the plate as Dotty refilled his coffee cup.

"Jake," I cautioned, "you'll be up all night."

Dotty set the coffee pot down and took her seat. "Did you catch the *Steve Allen Show* last night?" she asked as she scooped up her cards.

Jake rolled his eyes. "Did we ever! Could you believe that guy? What was his name again?"

"Presley." I passed three cards to Sam. "Elvis Presley."

"Elvis! Now I ask you, what kind of a name is Elvis?" Sam said.

"A dangerous one, I think," Jake said. "He had every girl in the place fainting on the floor with his gyrations. Even Libby, and she's eleven years old, for crying out loud!"

"Twelve, in two days," I corrected. "It's your bid."

"Six no trump."

"Thanks a lot, Jake Freeman," Dotty said with disgust. "Now

I can't bid. I have lots of help, Celia."

"No table talk, girls, you know the rules. Seven no trump."

"Sam! I have to pass too," I said. "Anyway, Jake had to tell Libby to quiet down, or else we'd turn off the TV."

"I know," Dotty chimed in. "We thought Rachel was going to faint, didn't we, Sam? The kids are already calling him 'Elvis the pelvis.' I think he's kind of cute."

"Dotty!"

"I don't see what the fuss is all about." Sam arched his eyebrows and took my king of hearts with the ace. "He's a fad. He'll wear himself out in a month."

Jake laughed. "Or buy some chiropractor a swimming pool."

"You're just jealous, Jake Freeman." Dotty gathered up the cards and gave the guys eight hundred points. "I bet you haven't been able to move like that in years."

We all laughed—including Jake, though not as long or as loud as everyone else. He smoothed his shirt down over the small paunch that had replaced his once-firm abdomen and sat up a little straighter in the chair. No one else noticed.

"Anyway," Dotty continued, "I agree with Sam: this Elvis is just a phase. Surely that music won't catch on. It's so loud and jumbled, you can't even understand the words."

"I believe he made some reference to a hound dog." Sam kept a straight face while the rest of us dissolved into laughter.

"What's so funny, Mom?"

"Yeah, what's so funny?"

Libby and Rachel sidled up to the table. Libby hung over her father's shoulder while Rachel snuggled on Sam's lap.

"You girls are supposed to be asleep." Dotty tried to look fierce, but it only made us all laugh harder.

Jake looked at his watch. "Sorry to break up this laugh fest, but it's time to go. It's already ten, and some of us have to work for a living."

Chapter Twenty-nine

"Carry me, Daddy?" Libby asked.

Jake groaned. "Not on your life. You're big enough to carry me." He ruffled her hair, then picked her up and tossed her over his shoulder. "Anyone want a sack of potatoes?" he teased. "They're sweet as sugar."

Libby squealed and giggled, while Rachel clung to Sam's pantleg and waved a sleepy good-by. The two girls seemed so young—still babies. And for a moment I wished they could stay that way forever.

As Jake pulled out of the driveway, I moved across the seat and laid my head against his shoulder. He smiled and slid his arm around my shoulder. "Tired?"

I shook my head. He grinned and pulled me closer, then drove one-handed all the way home.

Chapter
Thirty

On July 4, 1956, three days after Elvis Presley appeared on *The Steve Allen Show,* Libby turned twelve.

To celebrate, we had a wiener roast on the beach at Huntington Beach. They shot the fireworks from the pier just like every year, except this year they seemed brighter and bigger. They whistled and popped and shot spirals of diamond sparks into the night sky.

Libby and Rachel, with David and the twins in tow, wandered down to the tide line to watch the burned-out rockets sizzle and steam as they hit the water. Jake and I lay back on our blanket, tired and content. We were as sticky as the children from eating roasted marshmallows, but we held hands anyway and counted stars between each sparkling display.

Jake had come home every night that week and closed the shop the whole weekend, even though he could have stayed busy. "My girl only turns twelve once," he told Sam. "Besides, Celia and I need a holiday."

Whatever his reasons, I was glad to have him home. The day at the beach had been exhausting but fun. Libby was burnt to a crisp, of course. So were Rachel, David and the twins. Zeke was still afraid of the ocean waves. Dotty kept him close to her and under the umbrella, where he seemed content to dig with his shovel and bucket and bury the feet of any adult who would volunteer.

"Dotty sure has been quiet today," I whispered to Jake. "She hasn't moved from her blanket, and she didn't eat a bite at dinner."

I could feel Jake's muscles twitch in the darkness. He turned on his side and brushed sand from my hair with his fingertips. "Maybe she's just enjoying the rest. With five kids, I doubt she gets to lay around at home." He bent his head and kissed my shoulder.

"Jake, behave."

The sky lit up with the grand finale: an intricate pattern of red, white and blue lights that drew oohs and aahs from up and down the beach. I could see the light in Jake's eyes too. Mischief and hunger rolled into one. He was just about to kiss me, for real this time, when I felt someone tug on the blanket by my feet.

"Celia? Jake? Sorry, buddy." Sam stood over us, his arms laden with blankets and towels. "Dot and I are going to take off. My legs are cramping, and she says she's tired." He sounded concerned.

Jake pushed to his feet. "Let me help you get this stuff to the car. The kids should be back any minute."

The men set off toward the parking lot. I scanned the beach for Libby and the others, but all I could see was the flickering lights of dozens of campfires.

I crawled over to Dotty's blanket. She was packing the food basket, with little Zeke, wrapped tightly in a beach towel, curled next to her, sound asleep. "Need help?"

She shook her head. "Thanks anyway. The kids will be here in a minute. Rachel and David can get the rest of this stuff."

I looked around. Three sets of pails and shovels, a whiffle ball, a plastic bat and two large half-inflated beach balls decorated the sand for five feet in each direction. "How did they get it all down here?"

Dotty followed my gaze. "Remember, there's five of them. They have a lot of energy. Funny how it disappears when it's time to go home." She looked fondly at her youngest. An edge of the towel had crept over his nose; she pulled it back and sighed. "They grow up fast, don't they, Celia? It seems like yesterday he was in diapers, sucking on a bottle."

"Would you really want that again? I wouldn't. Not the diapers, anyway." I stood and scanned the crowd, most of whom were moving off the beach and toward the parking lot.

"Mom!" The trembling voice seemed to come out of nowhere. I jumped and saw Libby standing at the edge of the blanket. Her teeth were chattering, her shoulders shaking violently.

My heart lurched. "Libby, what's wrong?" I reached for her, but she pulled away and turned to Dot.

"J-J-Joe's hurt, Aunt Dotty," she said, trying to catch her breath. "You've got to come right now. I think he's hurt real bad."

I helped Dotty to her feet and steadied her as she almost dropped back down again. "Dotty Levi, don't you dare faint on me. I'll go. You stay here with Zeke. Send Jake and Sam as soon as you see them."

She didn't argue, but sank back down on the blanket. "Hurry, Celia. I don't know why I'm so dizzy."

"Mom, come on!" Libby grabbed my arm and pulled me toward the water. We hadn't run ten yards when I saw a crowd of people gathered. They parted to let us through. Jacob Joe sat propped against his brother David, while a white-faced Rachel cradled his foot in her lap. Someone had wrapped it in a towel, which I could see at a glance was already soaked with blood.

Sarah sat as close as she could get to her twin, sobbing and hanging onto his arm for dear life. Gasping for breath, I pried her away from him and handed her to Libby. "Take her back to Dotty."

Libby grabbed her with both arms and dragged her kicking and screaming down the beach.

Jacob Joseph's face was pale as ocean foam beneath his sunburn. He gritted his teeth but didn't make a sound.

Was he in shock? I racked my brain trying to remember what to do. Someone handed me a blanket, and I wrapped it around the shivering eight-year-old. Someone else knelt down and wound a roll of gauze around the blood-soaked towel. "We need to get him to a hospital," they said.

I nodded, but I couldn't move. It was as if I had frozen to the spot, my arms around Dotty's son. He was like my son too, for all the years I'd watched him grow. Then I heard Libby's voice. "Over here, Daddy!"

Sam and Jake were at my elbow. Sam picked up his child. "I'll drive," I heard Jake say. Then I heard my own voice, echoing from somewhere far away: "Come on, kids, let's go help your mother."

* * *

Jake got home at half-past midnight. I could tell he was exhausted. He was pale and trembling in spite of the heat.

"It was a mayonnaise jar. Can you believe that, Celia? Someone left a broken mayonnaise jar buried in the sand." Jake quit pacing, sat down on the sofa and buried his face in his hands. When he looked up, his eyes were red and swollen. More from anger, I thought, than tears.

I sat next to him and wiped the sweat from his face. "How is he?"

Jake arched his shoulders and fell back against the cushions, pulling me to rest against his chest. His shirt was damp, and from this position I noticed his Bermuda shorts were stained with blood. "He'll be okay. Sixteen stitches. The doc said he'd be out of commission for a while, but no major damage." He took a deep breath. "J's a brave kid. Only screamed once, when they pumped in the xylicaine. Dotty had to leave, though. She got sick twice."

"Poor Dot. It must be awful to have a child hurt that bad."

Jake nodded. "I guess she has a right to fall apart. But if you think about it, that's really not like her. She was a rag when we got her home. Are the others okay?"

"Yes, finally. They're all sleeping. I put Sarah in our bed between Libby and Rachel. It was the only way she'd go down. David and Zeke are in Libby's room."

Jake grimaced. "Where does that leave us?"

I smiled and patted the sofa. "Right here, partner. The best boarding house in town."

Chapter
Thirty-one

The next morning I suggested we go to the zoo, but Sarah was still too upset and David didn't have any clothes with him. Rachel borrowed an outfit from Libby, and Carol's mother drove them to the roller rink.

I took David, Zeke and Sarah home around ten. "How is he?" I asked when Dotty opened the door. "A better question: how are you?"

Dotty looked like death warmed over, as Mama would have said. Her tangled hair hung in strings around her shoulders; her eyes, dull and vacant behind swollen lids, stared somewhere over my head.

"J. Joe's fine. I feel terrible." She tried to grin and failed. "Hi, guys." She hugged David, then Zeke, who latched onto her like a monkey, then rushed up the stairs toward the boys' room. He nearly flattened Sarah, who stood with one hand on the doorsill, staring at her brother's bed.

"Where is he?" Zeke hollered. "I want to count the stitches."

"Ezekiel, Sarah—come down here and let your brother sleep."

"Aw, Mom." Zeke charged downstairs and raced toward the kitchen. "I want some corn flakes. Sarah, pour me some milk"— he looked at his mother—"please?"

Sarah ignored him and clung to her mother's leg like she'd been coated with Elmer's glue.

Dotty was fading fast. I poured Zeke's milk, then helped Dotty get Sarah settled with a book in the bed across from Jacob. Sarah seemed content to watch him sleep. "As long as she can see him she'll be fine," Dotty insisted. "Actually, she'll be a help. With her on guard, I can take a nap."

David appeared in the living room, hair combed and a wrapped gift under his arm. "May I have some money please, Mother? Ronald's parents are taking us to Disneyland for his birthday, and Dad said I could go." He stood there calmly, but I could tell by the tremor in his voice he was afraid she'd forgotten. I could also tell, by the look on Dotty's face, she had.

"Oh, grief. Sam, where are you when I need you?" she muttered and headed toward the bedroom. "I'll get my purse." She returned and handed David an envelope. "Your father must have remembered. Is it enough?"

David's eyes glowed as he thumbed through the cash. "Hey, wow! Yeah, it's great. I can go on the Matterhorn, the Tea Cups, the Jungle Ride—everything!" A horn honked outside. "It's them. Thanks, Mom!" He kissed her offered cheek and raced for the door.

He was halfway down the steps when he ran back and wrapped me in a rib-cracking hug. "Thanks, Aunt Celia, for taking care of us," he said. I would swear I saw a tear form before he raced away again.

Was this the same child who used to chase the girls with garden snakes? The one who almost failed first grade because "I was just having fun—I didn't know I *had* to learn to read"? Now, at nine years old, he was a treasure.

I'd take him home in a minute.

The thought surprised me. My intense longing for another child had fled somewhere around Libby's tenth birthday. Now

Chapter Thirty-one

I realized how much Sam and Dotty's children meant to me.

I collared Zeke on his way back into the boys' bedroom. "Wait for me, kiddo. We'll find some clean shorts and a shirt, then you can help me buy some groceries."

He looked dubious. "Can I steer the cart?"

I sighed and knew I'd think twice before I took this one home. He had too much energy for me.

* * *

It was after noon before I had time to call Aunt Rose. Her voice was cheerful, and she sounded more relaxed.

"Yes, we had a good weekend, dear. And your uncle started work again this morning. Officially, that is. He's been grateful for the work Jake sent his way, but he needed more to do. He's got four clients now and a nice office in the garage. It certainly makes a difference; he's happier than he's been in months."

I could tell Uncle Edward's improved disposition was working wonders on Aunt Rose, but I couldn't get past "the work Jake sent his way." I racked my brain but couldn't remember Jake saying a word about work for Uncle Edward. I didn't know about a new office either. "Are you sure it won't be too much for him?"

"It's just book work. He did it for years before he went into management at the plant. He needs to be busy, Cissy. He goes crazy just sitting around." She didn't say "he drives me crazy too," but I could hear it in her voice.

"Chuck is making so much progress. You'll be proud of him. His therapy is going well, and he doesn't give Anne near the fuss that he gave me. I think . . ."

I waited a moment, hearing nothing but silence. "What is it?"

"Oh, nothing. A silly notion. She's seven years older . . . Now, if their ages were reversed . . ." She was talking more to herself than me, but before I could interrupt she had changed the subject.

"How is little Jacob? Jake called last night to ask for prayer. The poor little thing. It must have been an ordeal for all of you."

I brought her up to date on J. Joe's injury, promised we'd come out next Sunday after church and hung up in a daze.

I walked over to the window and ran my hand across the dusty blinds. Zeke was racing up and down the sidewalk on his trike, singing at the top of his voice, "Praise him! Praise him! All ye little children." Suddenly he skidded to a halt and looked up at the sky. Face beaming, he closed his eyes against the noon-bright sun and let the warmth seep into his skin. I started to call him; the temperature was near ninety, and he could easily get a burn. But he was so intent, so centered on the moment . . .

For an instant my mind stopped whirling. The truth seeped in: I had to find my center too. I plopped down into Jake's easy chair.

Who was I? Jake's wife, certainly. Libby's mother, Chuck's sister and Dotty's friend. These roles had consumed me for years, and I had been content. Now I felt like they were eating me alive.

I was also my mother's daughter. That thought delighted and scared me by turns. Mama was a loving, caring person, but she went away, deserted us sure as if she'd run off to another world. I couldn't let that happen—not to me or to my family.

As I listened to the reassuring squeak of Zeke's tricycle wheels and his sweet, clear voice singing to the sun, I closed my eyes and sought a place of calm that I knew could only come from one source.

* * *

Sam came to collect Zeke that evening, more concerned for Dotty than he was for J. Joe. "She's really sick, Celia. She says it's just the flu, but I'm staying home tomorrow and taking them both to the doctor." He waved away my offer to keep the others. "Thanks for asking, but we could use Rachel and David's help at home. Sarah won't leave J. Joe's side, which is great. She keeps him entertained."

He hefted Zeke over his head to a sitting position on his shoulders. "As for this little monkey, he can help his old dad buy groceries. How about it, sport?" He grabbed Zeke's legs and pretended to gallop across the room. I winced at the pain I knew the effort caused, but Sam, as usual, hid it well.

"Yippee!" Zeke squealed. "I get to push the cart."

* * *

Jake didn't make it home for dinner, and my resolve to be more understanding melted like the whipped cream on his Jell-O. I stuck his plate in the Frigidaire. It took all my self-control not to snap at Libby when she asked for the thousandth time to spend the night at Carol's.

"Why not? You never let me do anything."

I took a deep breath and sat beside her on the sofa. "Because," I reminded her, "Carol's parents won't be home. I thought we had this settled."

"But Carol's brother will be there. I just found out. He's going to baby-sit because their sister Jenny's not old enough to stay alone."

I hoped my distress didn't show. If this was the same brother who taught Carol how to burn graffiti into lawns . . .

"Liberty Jane." I turned her face and looked into her eyes. "You may not spend the night at Carol's, and that's final."

Her eyes blazed, then lowered, defeated, to the floor. Without a word she stood and stomped into her room. I leaned back into the sofa pillows and stifled a sudden urge to laugh.

It's not funny, I wanted to shout to the heavens. *She's only twelve! How will we ever get through the next six years?*

* * *

Jake strolled through the back door at nine o'clock big as you please, slapped an envelope down on the counter and looked around the kitchen like he was surprised his dinner wasn't steaming on the stove. "What's to eat, babe? I'm starved."

I wanted to clobber him. Instead I pointed toward the fridge. "Cold roast beef and potatoes." He looked blank, then pulled his chair out from the table. I started to say, "Wash your hands before you sit," but I noticed they were already clean.

"Where have you been, Jake Freeman? I was worried to death when you didn't call."

He grinned, snatched up the envelope and slid it under his napkin. "Food first, woman, then the surprise."

He looked pleased with himself, like a cat who'd just cleaned out a nest of mice. Did he expect me to pet and praise him? I fumed inwardly while I sliced the meat and got out bread for sandwiches. I fried the cold potatoes and set the meal in front of Jake. He looked wounded when I didn't return his smile.

"I think there's something steaming besides the vegetables." It seemed nothing could destroy his cheerful mood, but he didn't give me a chance to try. "I've been thinking," he said between bites of sandwich. "You've been so cross—" He caught himself. "Uh, tired lately. I thought it would do us both some good to get away, so . . ." He pulled out the envelope and handed it to me with a flourish. "This, madam, is for you."

I lifted the flap and pulled out a square of white paper with blue lines and the word RECEIPT stenciled across the top. The fancy script that flowed across the page made my heart dance. Bear Creek Lodge, 2 days, 1 night for two, $25.00 paid in full.

"Oh Jake," I felt my eyes tear up, "do you mean it?" I looked closer. "It's for this weekend."

He swallowed his last bite of potato and pulled me to his lap. "Don't worry about it, Celia. Everything's arranged."

"Hi, Daddy." Libby bounded into the kitchen and peered over her father's shoulder. "Wow, Bear Lake, cool. Can I bring Rachel or Carol?"

Jake smiled and slid his free arm around her waist. "Sorry, sugar, not this time. Your mother and I need to get away."

It took a minute for the news to register. I expected a storm of tears, but Libby just nodded. "Oh, right." She rolled her eyes and kissed her father on the cheek. " 'Night, Mom. 'Night Daddy. I'm going to bed."

I looked at the clock. Nine-thirty. She was up to something. "Jake," I started, "we can't—"

His lips stopped me.

"She's staying with Ed and Rose," he said when we could breathe again. "It's all arranged."

* * *

We checked in on Libby on our way to bed. She was curled up on her side, one arm under the pillow cradling her head, the other wrapped around it, like she used to hug her Gretel doll.

She hadn't played with dolls in years, unless you counted paper ones. Even those, I realized, had been discarded. Replaced by books and friends and roller skates. Soon it would be boys.

I felt an instant sense of loss, an emptiness I couldn't explain. I looked at Jake. His face, as he stared at our daughter, held wonder and sadness and love. He took my hand and led me out into the hall, shutting the door behind us. He tipped my chin and looked deep into my eyes. "They have to, you know."

"Have to what?"

"Grow up. That's the way God designed it. And when all is said and done, we will still have us. You and me forever."

"Promise?" I felt my chin begin to tremble.

He pulled me close and held me quiet for a long, long time. "Till death," he whispered.

Chapter
Thirty-two

Bear Lake was a purple mirror reflecting the setting sun. The air smelled of cedar and pine. It brought back good memories. Bad ones too, of course, but the new Bear Creek Lodge was on the other side of the lake from where Papa's enemies had tried to lead me to my death.

I shuddered at the memory of Stiles's grip on my arm. The stench of tobacco smoke and motor oil still made me nauseous. I couldn't help but think that except for the grace of God, who gave me a way to escape, I would be dead.

I felt Jake's arm circle my shoulders and draw me close. The sunset we had been admiring faded to a tinge of purple across the darkening sky. A nighthawk called, then silence closed in around us until our own breathing sounded loud in our ears.

"I'm glad we have tomorrow," Jake whispered. "One day's not enough."

I was loath to break the silence, so I nodded my agreement. We stood awhile longer in the deepening dark and counted the lights of campfires across the lake. We were standing on the balcony, just outside the door to our room. Inside a cold supper of cheese and bread and fruit was laid out on a small wrought-iron table.

It had been a day made in heaven: warm and balmy, inviting us to walk and explore for hours, talking about everything and nothing. By the time we came back to our room, I remembered why I had fallen in love with this man. The things that drew me to him in the first place—his self-assurance, his cocky grin, the slight swagger when he walked—could rankle at times, but in the right time and place I still found them alluring. As he led me in to supper, I vowed to tell him so.

* * *

We checked out Sunday at noon and drove the thirty miles back to San Bernardino in silence, each lost in our own thoughts. I was wishing our holiday could have gone on a few days longer. Jake told me later he was thinking the same thing.

"One of these days, we'll take a real vacation," he said. "When the business is built up a bit and I can afford to hire someone to fill in." He kissed me on the cheek. "Two weeks of fun and sun, I promise!"

Aunt Rose had fixed fried chicken, mashed potatoes and gravy, and oven-warm apple pie. Jake covered his plate with his napkin when she tried to slip him another piece of pie. "Rose-bud, if I didn't know better, I'd swear you were trying to make me explode. Better watch it, Chuck. If she has her way, you'll be fat as a Christmas turkey in no time."

Chuck grinned and patted his washboard-flat stomach. "I have filled out some, haven't I? The women in this house spoil me." He glanced at Anne Marie, who lowered her head and concentrated on her last bite of crust. Chuck leaned back in his chair. "Yep, a man could get used to this."

* * *

"She was blushing," I told Jake later. "I'd swear to it. Do you think there could be anything to it? I mean, Aunt Rose seems to think they might be attracted to each other."

Jake shrugged. "I suppose it's possible, but nothing will come of it, Celia. They're too different. Besides, Anne is seven—no, almost eight years older. She'd never go for someone like your brother."

"What do you mean, 'someone like my brother'?" I asked. But Jake suddenly had something to do in the garage.

* * *

My hours at Children's Charities had crept up steadily over the past few months, but if Jake noticed, he didn't seem to mind. On Tuesday I worked six hours straight, typing forms and reading the file on an eighteen-year-old girl living at an unwed mothers' home in Santa Monica. The girl's parents had kicked her out, and she had no means of supporting herself and her child. Social Services thought they had found a good match for the baby, parents with the same physical characteristics and a steady income, but the baby would need a foster home while the lengthy adoption process was completed.

Mr. Johnson had brought the file in that morning and set it on my desk. "You've studied enough of these now, Celia; think you can handle this one yourself?"

I smiled and nodded, but by that evening I was having second thoughts. What if I made the wrong choice? The poor little baby would have enough adjusting to do; I had to pick a stable home where he'd be loved as well as sheltered.

The bus was crowded, and I had to stand all the way home. While the other passengers jostled for vacated seats, I wrestled with my decision, plagued by memories of Chuck and Baby Grace. By the time I got dinner on the table, I felt foggy-headed and exhausted.

"Guess whose car I fixed today," Jake asked, brandishing a forkful of Salisbury steak. "Leo Ferguson's!"

I dropped my napkin and stared at him while he calmly chewed and swallowed the meat.

"Came in right at eleven-thirty. Wouldn't look me in the eye, but told me he'd lost the brakes on his Pontiac at the corner of Wells and Valley Boulevard. He could pump 'em some, so he drove on and my shop was the first one in sight."

Jake cut up another bite of steak and dipped it in his mashed potatoes. I looked at Libby, but she was busy pushing peas around her plate and didn't notice.

"Had a young woman and a little boy in the car."

I had seen the girl and the little one walking to the Frosty Freeze. I'd waved and called out "hi," but the girl just dropped her head like she was counting cracks in the sidewalk. I waited for Jake to go on, but he was intent on mopping up gravy with his last piece of bread.

"Well?" I prompted.

"Well, what?"

"You know very well what! Who in the world are they?"

"I didn't ask." Jake drained his milk, wadded up his napkin and tossed it on his empty plate. "He actually thanked me for fixing the car. I didn't want to be too nosy."

"I know," Libby interjected.

The words were garbled, and I switched my stare across the table to our daughter. "Liberty Jane, please swallow your food before you talk."

She gulped down a mouthful of potatoes. "That's Mr. and Mrs. Ferguson's daughter. She cleans house sometimes for Carol's mother. Carol says the baby's a bastard, but I think he's cute."

You could have cut the silence with a knife. Libby must have realized what she'd said, because she turned three shades of purple and covered her mouth with her hand.

I couldn't think what to say. Jake told me later my mouth dropped to my knees. Then we all found our voices at once.

Libby mumbled something about bedtime and asked to be excused.

Her father said, "Wait a minute, young lady, what else do you know?" I sputtered, "Not before you clean your plate. Don't you know there are children starving in China?"

* * *

Dotty called on Wednesday morning at half-past nine. Her voice sounded thick, like she was talking around a mouthful of cotton. "Celia, I need you. Can you come over?"

"Dotty, what's wrong? Is it Jacob?"

"No," she said, "it's me. Please, Cissy, I need to talk to you." I almost asked if she'd been drinking, but I knew that wasn't true.

She'd been crying though. I knew it the minute I walked in the door. She looked up from the couch, where she was folding laundry into a wicker basket. "Hi." She tried a smile, but it came out a grimace instead.

I sat down next to her and took her hands in my own. She squeezed my fingers in reassurance and took a deep breath. "I just talked to the nurse at Dr. Baker's office. She said the rabbit died."

I was stunned, "Dorothy Levi, you can't be pregnant, you're over thirty!"

She nodded. "I know. Thirty-four. It's not possible. It has to be the flu. I tried to tell that to the nurse. Argued with her for fifteen minutes before she finally put the doctor on the phone." She gulped. "He swears it's true. He ran some other tests and they're conclusive. Oh, Cissy, what am I going to do?"

* * *

The sisters Livermore and Wagington had a field day.

Dotty hadn't shared her secret with anyone but Jake and me. And Sam, of course. He had been elated with the news. "Zeke is getting much too big to carry. I need a baby to tote around; it keeps the strength up in my leg muscles."

We all knew that was a farce. Sam had worked out with

weights since the day he got out of the hospital sixteen years ago. He rarely missed a day. The doctors were amazed and admitted that exercise had probably been the key to his recovery. "That and a lot of prayer," Sam had told them.

One Sunday morning, two weeks after we had heard the news, Dr. Baker's nurse, Miss Fowler, came up to Dotty after the morning church service. "Dorothy, how are you feeling?" She smiled and put an arm around Dotty's shoulders. "You mustn't fret now, dear. It's not good for the baby. You'll be fine. Doctor has handled several of these late-in-life pregnancies."

Unfortunately, Mrs. Edna Livermore was standing right behind the two of them.

"I swear her ears swelled up to twice their size," I told Jake later. "And you should have seen her eyes. They bulged like she'd just swallowed a peppercorn. She actually ran across the vestibule and dragged her sister, Eunice, to that cubbyhole under the stairs. It didn't take any imagination to guess what she was telling her. Now it will be all over church."

"More like all over the state." Jake chuckled. "So what? Why does it have to be some deep dark secret? Dotty's not ashamed of it, is she?"

"Of course she's not ashamed! But mark my words, those two busybodies will find a way to twist it."

Sure enough, by Saturday afternoon three people had called me to ask, "Is it true Dorothy and Sam Levi might have to sell their house to pay for this baby? I mean, with all those mouths to feed."

"Honestly, Jake, the rumor mill has them in the poorhouse. The pastor's wife even asked if I thought Dotty would like to go through the missionary barrel for clothes. We have to put a stop to this."

"How?" Jake kissed my cheek and turned on the ball game.

"Trust me, babe, these things die down faster if you just let them go."

* * *

Mary Margaret chose that next Sunday to come back to church.

"Well, praise the Lord and lock up the offering, Celia." Jake's elbow poked my ribs. "Look who just came in the door."

I couldn't believe my eyes. She had on a white blouse with a Peter Pan collar, a navy-blue short-sleeved jacket and a matching skirt that came all the way below her knees.

She looked everywhere but toward the back, where we were sitting on the end of the last row just in case Dotty had to leave in a hurry. I stood up and started to wave her over, but the music began and the choir filed in, so I had to sit down.

Mary Margaret took one more quick look around, then planted herself in the closest vacant seat. Halfway through the second song I realized that she was sitting right in front of Miss Wagington and Mrs. Livermore. I nearly dropped my hymnal. I was so nervous, I didn't hear a word of the sermon. By the time Pastor Willis said the final amen, I had conjured up all sorts of terrible consequences resulting from Mary Margaret's choice of a seat.

Either the sisters didn't recognize her or they were still intent on destroying Sam and Dotty's bank account. I do know that immediately after the congregation was dismissed, they were in deep discussion with the two women to Edna's left. Several people had to ask them to step aside so they could exit the row.

Mary Margaret had stopped searching the audience for a familiar face. She didn't even pretend to be studying the bulletin. She kept her head high and her ears open and evidently heard every word the "old biddies," as she called them, had to say.

It took Jake and me a few minutes to work our way in that direction. By the time we were in helloing distance, I noticed M had turned around. I never did hear what she said, and no one else would tell me. I only know that when I reached the group, the sisters were both the color of overripe tomatoes.

One of the women they had been talking to was staring open-mouthed at my cousin, fanning herself with the bulletin. The other, a woman about my age, yanked on her sleeve, trying to pull her into the aisle.

Mary Margaret's face was serene and plastered with the sweetest smile. A crocodile smile, Papa would have called it. And the glint in her eyes told me she had chewed them up and swallowed them for dinner.

"Ladies," Jake made a half-bow toward the sisters, trying to draw their attention away from M. It worked. Sputtering and huffing, Mrs. Livermore fussed with the flowers on her hat while Miss Wagington collected their bags. They marched out of the church without a backward glance and without speaking to another soul.

Later, Pastor Willis said it was the best thing that could have happened to them.

Chapter
Thirty-three

By Wednesday morning I was beginning to wish Mr. Bell had never invented the telephone. I'd had four or five calls a day from friends saying how wonderful it was to see Mary Margaret in church, and "by the way, whatever did she say to make Edna and Eunice hustle off like that? They didn't say another word to a single soul."

My answer was always the same: "Yes, we're so glad Mary Margaret has decided to come back," and "No, I'm sorry, but I have no idea what she said."

Finally I couldn't stand it any longer, so I called M as soon as I knew she was home from work and out of the bath.

"Let's just say I suggested that rumormongers usually wind up biting their own tongues."

"M—"

"Leave it, Celia."

"Well, we are glad to have you back, you know that. We'll save you a seat next Sunday."

"Don't bother," she said. "Not that I don't want your company. I just think I'll sit close to those flapping-jawed busybodies and be their conscience for a while."

Mary Margaret's tone held more than a hint of humor. What

had gotten into her? I wanted more than anything to ask what had brought her back to church, but I was afraid to rock the boat.

The line was quiet long enough to make me think she might have hung up. "Well, aren't you going to ask why I came back?"

"It doesn't matter, M," I said quickly. "We're just glad—"

"It does matter, Celia. It's obvious that Mother and Daddy prefer saints to sinners. So do you and Jake, and your brother, Chuck."

Another pause, but my head was too full to think of what to say. What did she mean about Chuck? Then it hit me. She was jealous—jealous of Anne Marie! "Oh, M," I said gently. She pretended not to hear.

"Besides," she went on, "if I want to spend time with my niece, I need to get my act together, don't I?" Her voice was quiet and sad, with a hint of defiance that dared me to deny it.

I didn't.

"So what if her motives aren't pure?" Jake said later. "At least she's hearing the truth. It has to seep in sometime."

* * *

It wasn't long before we learned the truth about the Fergusons. Like I told Jake later, "It just goes to show we should never judge someone. You never know what's happened to make them the way they are."

I had had to call Carol's mother to get permission for Carol to stay for dinner. I was dying to ask what she knew about the Fergusons' daughter, but pictures of Edna and Eunice intruded on my conscience, so I bit my tongue and hung up the phone.

Not two minutes later, she called back.

"I'm sorry, Celia, but I forgot to ask you if you know anyone who needs help with housecleaning. I have a girl who's helped me a few times, a sweet young thing, and she needs the money desperately. Actually I think she lives just down the street from you."

I learned that the "sweet young thing" was the Fergusons' twenty-year-old daughter, Diane. She had gotten "in the family way" when she was seventeen. They'd sent her off to live with an aunt somewhere in Washington, then moved themselves to escape the shame of it.

"I guess they were afraid someone would find out," I told Jake later that night. "That's why they kept to themselves so much."

Jake nodded. "That would explain the bad temper too. He probably wants to murder the guy."

We decided to go out of our way to be a little nicer to the Fergusons.

* * *

I almost didn't answer the phone on Thursday morning. The sun was already sucking up moisture from our just-watered flowerbeds, and I wanted to get the wash on the line before the temperature hit 100. But I couldn't stand to let a ringing phone go unanswered. What if it were Jake or Libby calling? Or something wrong with Dotty and the baby? By the time I caught it on the seventh ring, I had conjured up all sorts of emergencies, but I never would have guessed how important the call really was. Never in a million years.

"Mrs. Freeman?" The voice in my ear was quiet, almost a whisper, and I had to hold my breath to understand. "This is Florence DuVal. Please don't hang up. I know you must hate me, but I have to talk to you. Please?"

I was stunned. Before I could get my tongue untied, she rushed on. "I know it's inconvenient, but I really can't talk long on the phone. Would it be okay . . . I mean, could we meet somewhere? Maybe Sunday? I'm only at school a few more days, and . . ."

Somewhere in the background I heard a door slam and a deep

male voice call out, "Hey, Flo, what's the holdup?"

"Look, I gotta go. I'll call you later. Bye."

"Florence, wait! I—" But the line droned its dial tone in my ear.

I wanted to tell her it wasn't like she thought. What had she said? "I know you must hate me." I wanted her to know that wasn't true.

At least she wanted to meet me. *Don't get your hopes up,* I chided myself, *she probably just wants to tell you to "get lost," once and for all.*

I had all afternoon to stew. By the time Libby came home from school, the laundry was off the line and folded, and every room in the house sparkled. I almost set up the ironing board, but a blast of heat from the open front door convinced me to let it wait till morning. I grabbed Libby and measured her for the new dress pattern I'd bought, but when I tried to sew, I couldn't sit still and had to tear a seam out three times.

"Only a few more days," she'd said. Tomorrow was Friday. If we were to meet on Sunday, we'd have to arrange it soon. But what if something scared her off and she never called back? I had no idea how to get in touch with her.

Or did I? I might not have a phone number, but hadn't she said she was at school? The USC campus was only a few miles from our new Children's Charities office. *And,* my mind was racing a mile a minute, *I'm scheduled to work tomorrow.*

The thought made my skin prickle, but when Florence still hadn't called by bedtime, I made up my mind. Tomorrow, Celia Marie Freeman, who had never been on a college campus in her life, was going to USC to find her sister.

* * *

The University of Southern California was a private school, not as prestigious as Stanford or Berkeley, but from what Dr. DuVal had said, it had been Florence's choice.

Chuck had found that information hilarious. "Man," he had laughed when his father left the room, "I bet that really fried his bacon! The old man started preaching Berkeley as soon as Flo was out of diapers. He never forgave me for not going there; he must have had a coronary when Flo rebelled."

He coughed and clutched his stomach, then settled back on his pillows, grinning up at me. "Our sister always did have a stubborn streak. I bet she chose USC because of some boy."

I got off the bus a block from the school. The campus was a warren of buildings and cement walkways dominated by a huge statue of a Trojan warrior. The streets were lined with palm trees, their fronds drooping in the hot wind. I felt like a very small mouse in a very large maze. I had no idea how I'd find my sister.

I'd worn my summer suit: a blue skirt, a white cotton blouse and a blue linen jacket that was already wet under the arms. I itched to take it off, and my nylons and heels as well.

I stepped off the sidewalk into the shade of a eucalyptus tree and watched the parade of students, the girls in suits and heels very much like mine, the boys in open-necked shirts with button-down collars and lightweight slacks.

I shook my head. "What must this place be like during the regular school year?"

"A zoo. Complete with every kind of animal known to man."

Startled, I grabbed a tree branch for support. The voice that had come from behind the tree materialized into a lean, long-limbed man who, with his crew cut and cocky grin, looked young enough to be a student. On second glance, I realized he was more the professor type, with a loosened tie and a corduroy jacket thrown across his leather briefcase.

"You look lost."

I realized I was staring and lowered my eyes to the sprinkler-wet lawn. I hadn't noticed it was wet before, and the dampness had already muddied my heels. The toes of his leather-fringed loafers were muddy too. Somehow I found that reassuring.

"Not lost." I looked up again. The grin was still there, and I decided to trust him. "I'm looking for my sister." I motioned to the congested landscape. "I didn't realize it would be this big."

He laughed and mopped sweat from the back of his neck with a monogrammed handkerchief. "Maybe I can help. What's your sister's name?"

"Florence. Florence DuVal."

His smile widened. "Hey, you're in luck. I have Florence in one of my classes. She stayed on this summer to finish an art history project." He paused. "Funny, I don't remember Flo mentioning a sister." His brow wrinkled, like Jake's always did when he was trying to solve a puzzle.

I held my breath. What if he didn't believe me? Would he think I meant her harm and call security? I wanted to run, but his hand on my elbow stopped me.

"Your timing's good. The cafeteria opened ten minutes ago. She's probably eating lunch. Come on."

His grip on my elbow tightened as he led me back to the sidewalk across the street and down a narrow alley. My heart was pounding, and by the time he realized I was running to keep up with him, I was truly out of breath.

"Sorry." The grin was back, and he slowed his pace to match mine. Then he stopped abruptly. "How rude of me! I haven't even introduced myself." He bent at the waist in a comic bow. "Stuart Haley, at your service, ma'am."

I took a deep breath and shook his offered hand. "Celia Freeman. It's nice to meet you, Mr. Haley."

Chapter
Thirty-four

By the time I tucked Libby in that night and slipped into my coolest summer nightgown, the whole day seemed like a dream. Or an Academy Award-winning movie that had held me spellbound all afternoon, then sent me spinning back to real life.

Jake moaned when I pulled back the sheet. "Man, am I beat. And I've got an interview first thing in the morning." His kiss connected just above my right ear. "Supposed to be a crack mechanic, and his references sounded good. If he checks out, I'll have someone to cover for me evenings and Saturdays. How'd you like that?"

When I assured him I'd like that fine, he yawned contentedly and rolled to his own side of the bed.

I sighed and folded my arms behind my head, glad to be left to my own thoughts. Had I really eaten lunch with a man named Stuart Haley and made a date to meet Florence at the zoo? It was all so unreal. Yet I knew every movement, every word of it was true. I could still smell the French fries and see the rings from narrow-bottomed glasses that had stained the wooden table.

We'd pushed our way into the cafeteria. "There they are." Stuart pointed to a slip of a girl and a well-built young man of about twenty-one stacking their empty trays on a rack by the far exit. "Florence, Jerry, wait up!" Stuart called out, his voice carrying across the room.

They turned around, and the look on Florence's face would have scared a ghost. She grabbed her boyfriend's arm, and for a minute I didn't know if she would faint or run.

The red-gold hair fell smoothly to narrow shoulders and turned under in a pageboy that outlined her narrow heart-shaped face. I would have known her anywhere; she looked so much like Krista, it took my breath away.

She stood stock-still, and I knew she recognized me too.

Stuart didn't seem to notice Flo's hesitation or my quick intake of breath, and the other diners kept up their incessant chatter as he propelled me across the room.

I have to give her credit: Florence held her ground. By the time we came up to them, her sunburnt, freckled face looked composed, even though her grip on Jerry's arm was causing her knuckles to turn white. He pulled free, slid a protective arm around her shoulders and nodded silently to Stuart. All the while his eyes never left my face, and I knew he understood exactly who I was.

"Celia." She looked from me to Stuart Haley. "How did you get here? I mean, what are you doing—?"

Stuart didn't blink an eye. "I work here, Miss DuVal, re-member? I found your sister wandering around like a poor lost waif and took it upon myself to help her locate you." He flashed me a grin and looked enormously pleased with himself.

Florence couldn't seem to find her voice again, and my re-solve had collapsed like a punctured balloon. After what seemed like an eternity, Stuart cleared his throat. "Well, Jerry, why don't we leave these two alone? Come on, I'll spring for a Coke."

"No." Florence grabbed Jerry's arm in a death grip, and I could tell by the poor boy's face he didn't know what to do.

I took a deep breath. "It's okay, Jerry, you can stay. This will only take a moment."

I faced my sister square-on and tried to keep my voice gentle. "You called me, Flo, remember? We have to talk. You know that."

She looked around the cafeteria like a frightened two-year-old. "Not here."

"All right. Where?"

She hesitated. "How about the zoo? You know those benches by the entrance, right by the flamingo ponds?"

"I've been there many times."

"Good." She sounded relieved. "Would Sunday work? I mean Sunday afternoon, around two o'clock? It's really the only time I have free."

I didn't have to think. "Sunday is fine."

"I'll see you then. Bye." She flicked one hand in Mr. Haley's direction and practically shoved Jerry through the double doors.

I leaned forward and watched them stride across the lawn and into a building on the other side.

"Arts and Science. Their project is due this afternoon," Stuart explained. "Come on," he said, leading me to an empty table. "I don't know about you, but I still want a Coke."

The funny thing was, he did nothing to stop me from saying, "Thank you, but I have to catch my bus." Which is what I fully intended to say. Only the next thing I knew, I was sitting across from him, munching a hamburger and sipping an ice-cold cola.

"It was the strangest thing," I told Dotty the next morning. "I don't even remember how much I told him. I know we talked about Grace, and Chuck too. He agreed that we should all meet. 'Get it all out in the open,' he said. 'You'll all feel better when it's done.' "

Chapter Thirty-four

"Is he a psych professor?" Dotty sounded skeptical.

"He's a graduate student. Teaches freshman English."

Dotty sighed. "Sometimes you scare me, girl. Oh, well, I agree you need to get this thing with Grace over with once and for all. Although I doubt it will be that simple. These things never are."

She was right, of course.

* * *

I had no intention of telling Jake about my visit to USC. Like my trip with Dotty to the park, I was sure he'd never understand, just scold me for taking such a chance and forbid me to do it again. Not that I ever would. But something inside of me rebelled at the thought of my husband telling me I couldn't.

I had to tell him about the phone call, though. If I was going to meet Grace on Sunday, I needed his cooperation and he'd want to know why.

Jake came home at noon on Saturday in a good mood. "The interview went great," he said, giving me a kiss and flinging his work cap in the direction of the service porch. "We now have an official employee."

He managed to tell me about it through two grilled-cheese sandwiches and half a can of vegetable-beef soup. I slipped a plate of fresh apple pie in next to his coffee cup. "Wow, pie in the afternoon—and it isn't even Sunday! What's up?"

"Oh, you." I cuffed his shoulder, but I couldn't hide my smile. I never could bluff this man. He knew me too well.

I told him about the phone call from Florence DuVal. "We talked again later," I improvised, "and she suggested we meet at the zoo on Sunday afternoon."

"And you agreed, just like that?" He was incredulous. "Well, you certainly can't go alone. She could be up to anything."

"Oh Jake, no. It's not like that. I'm sure she just wants to talk about Chuck or something," I finished lamely. In truth, I realized I didn't know what she had really wanted when she called.

"She could be angry enough to try something stupid. I'll take you," he decided. I left it at that.

"Actually I'm glad he's going," I confided to Dotty. "I don't think I can face Florence DuVal alone. Even if she is my sister."

* * *

That night we took Libby out to spend the night at Uncle Edward's. Once again the dinner table was set for eight, but Mary Margaret called at the last minute to say she couldn't make it.

"She has a date," Aunt Rose said. She set a plate of rolls on the table and called the men in from the living room. "Please turn off the TV and come to dinner, Edward. That game will still be on when we're done." There were groans from all three of them, but they obeyed—persuaded, I suppose, by the smell of Aunt Rose's roasted chicken and rosemary potatoes.

"So who's her date with?" Libby pounced into her chair and yanked her napkin into her lap.

"I don't know, dear," Aunt Rose smiled at her, "I didn't ask."

"I hope it's Michael, he's cool."

I had no idea how she knew about the men Mary Margaret dated, let alone a thing about their character. She started to say more, but I frowned and shook my head as Jake and the others appeared at the table. She folded her hands in mock piety and waited for Uncle Edward to say grace.

Chapter
Thirty-five

After dinner Jake and Uncle Edward went back to their base-ball game, but Anne Marie helped Chuck negotiate the steps down to the patio. "Come sit, Celia," she called back over her shoulder. "I haven't had a chance to talk with you in ages."

Chuck used his crutches like second arms, and I marveled at how much progress he'd made since his release from the hospital last November. The swelling on his face and head had disappeared, leaving a few scars that plastic surgery had not been able to repair; the scar from Papa's ring was one of them. His hair had grown back thick and straight, and white instead of blond. The doctors said his left eyelid would always droop, but his vision was fine, and his mind and memory were perfectly clear.

Like Sam, Chuck had tackled his physical therapy with a vengeance, working like a madman to build the muscles in his arms. His hips and legs were weaker, thin and spindly in spite of daily exercises that left him panting and white with pain.

"It'll come," Anne insisted. "Just don't give up." And with her patient coaxing, he continued to fight.

"It's an uphill battle, Cissy," he said. "But I'm gonna do it." He smiled ruefully. "I can't let everybody down, now can I?"

What about yourself, Chuck? I wanted to ask him. *You don't want to let yourself down either.* But I let it be. Self-esteem was another uphill battle for my brother, and Anne Marie seemed to be working on that as well.

We chatted for a while about Libby and Jake, then I asked Anne how her parents were. "They're okay," she sighed. "Davy—I mean Dave—is giving them fits, though. He keeps cutting school, and I know he's drinking." She picked up Chuck's left hand and began massaging it with both of her own. I noticed his platinum ring was missing.

"It's that crowd he hangs out with." She looked at me earnestly. "He's really a neat kid, just mixed up right now. I had hoped they could nip this in the bud before he goes off the deep end, but Pa doesn't seem to know how to deal with it." Her fingers stopped kneading Chuck's knuckles, but I noticed she didn't let go of his hand.

I felt guilty. It had been two months since we'd been over there. Jake had tried with Dave too, but had gotten nowhere. "Bug off," his brother had screamed, "I don't need another pa." So Jake had backed off.

"It was either that or deck him," Jake said. Later I think he wished he had.

Aunt Rose appeared and handed Chuck and me each a glass of lemonade. "Don't stay in the sun too long, dear," she said and kissed Chuck on the cheek. "Anne Marie, your mother is on the phone. Jake's talking to her now, but I'm sure she'd like to visit with you as well."

Anne excused herself and followed Aunt Rose into the house. I swished the ice cubes around the inside of my glass. Some of the liquid splashed on my dress. I brushed at the droplets and felt the folded paper I'd tucked into the skirt pocket. I pictured the neat lettering that marched across the envelope like tiny stick figures in a drawing: "Charles Byron Summers, Junior."

Mama had never called him that, at least not that I'd heard, but I guess in her mind the letters were official, like a birth certificate or marriage license. Or a last will and testament.

I had determined to pull the envelope from its hiding place and give it to Chuck right then, but he broke the silence before I could follow through.

"There was a girl, you know." He began as he always did when talking about the past: out of the clear blue, like we were in the middle of a conversation instead of at the beginning. It had taken me some time to get used to it, but by now I knew to just be still and listen. Chuck would get around to his point in his own good time.

He set his glass on one of the TV trays Aunt Rose used for patio tables. "Her name was Donna. We met at a Y dance one of my friends had dragged me to. I was working at the diner then and staying with this friend in a mop-closet room over his folks' garage. He'd met this chick at the dance the week before and wanted to go back, but he didn't want to go alone. So I figured, 'What the h-hey; I owe him.' He was letting me share his digs for free.

"Anyway, Donna walked in about ten o'clock and *wham!* right between the eyes. I thought she was the greatest thing since Kool-Aid. A real looker. Long blonde hair curled on the ends just below her shoulders. And those eyes, wide and blue as Mama's china saucers."

He must have seen the startled look in my eyes. "Yeah, I remember them. Not the flowered ones, but the blue ones she kept for company in Pike. I remember because she wouldn't ever let me touch them. Of course that made me want to all the more."

He grinned and went on with his story. "Anyway, Donna was a looker, and a talker too. She could charm the shirt off your back if she wanted to. And could she sing." He whistled long and low. "That night I sat there in a trance for hours, until they put the mike away and asked us to leave.

"Bill and his girl were long gone. He'd already slipped me a fiver and asked me to find someplace else to stay that night. I didn't care, really, I was used to crashing anywhere convenient. Even spent a night or two on the street."

He shifted his weight onto his right hip and took a sip of lemonade. I could see the pain flood his eyes, then disappear as if he'd simply willed it away. "It was just Donna and me. I wound up at her place." He looked at me for the first time since he'd started the story and shrugged. "I know you don't approve, but that's how it was.

"I stayed with her all winter. I had my job at Stobbie's, and she sang nights at clubs around the city. We lived pretty good. Food on the table and a bed. Didn't need much more than that."

He went quiet, somewhere inside himself. I didn't want to intrude on his reverie, but I didn't want him to stop talking either. Whether or not I approved, I wanted to hear about my brother's life. I knew so little beyond what he'd written in that horrible notebook.

I thought of the platinum wedding band. "Did you marry her?"

"No." I could tell his smile was forced. "I wanted to, but she didn't want a commitment right then. She insisted we wait. 'Until we get to know each other better,' she said." He shrugged. "I thought I knew her well enough. As it turned out, I didn't know her at all."

I heard the back door slam, and Anne Marie came to stand beside Chuck. "Am I interrupting?"

"No." His smile this time was genuine. He reached for her hand and drew her down beside him. "You've heard all this before."

"Don't stop on my account then. Celia has a right to know."

Chapter Thirty-five

He winced, but turned back to the conversation.

"To make a long story short, I wound up in Korea. Hadn't been there three months when I got Donna's Dear John letter." He shrugged again. "You know the routine."

I looked at Anne Marie. I wondered what she thought of Chuck's escapades, but her face registered only compassion. And something else I wouldn't even try to guess. It dawned on me that Aunt Rose's speculation must be right. Chuck and Anne's relationship had grown past nurse and patient.

"Korea was a hellhole. There's no other word for it. We either fried or froze our b—toes off. The Commies were a pack of yellow-belly curs, but there were more of them and they had bigger guns. We ran." He shook his head like he still couldn't believe it. "Wound up licking our wounds in a rat hole called Pusan. We held the dogs at bay until MacArthur sent in the Marines, then we ripped Seoul right out of their jaws."

He closed his eyes and leaned his head back against the metal chair. "It didn't come easy. A lot of guys died. Bill, for one. I heard later he got it at Inchon." His eyelids flicked twice, and he sat still, dry-eyed and silent in the late-afternoon sun.

Blood, guns and death. I'd heard it before: from Jake, from my cousin Billy's letters. I could tell by the way Anne Marie studied the cracks on the patio cement that she had seen her share in the Philippines.

"How could he let it happen?" Chuck asked.

"Who?"

"God." Chuck slammed his fist on the chair arm hard enough to knock it loose. He looked straight at Anne Marie. "If God's so loving and powerful, why didn't he put a stop to it?

"I killed two men—boys, really; they couldn't have been over seventeen. I looked in their faces. I saw the fear in their eyes and the hate. But it was either them or me, so I gunned them down."

He was breathing hard, his hands balled into fists. I thought he might strike out, but he clutched the arms of his chair instead and kept his eyes glued on Anne.

"There were only a few ways to forget. You know? I tried them all: the booze, the drugs, the women. It messed up my head. I don't know . . ."

I couldn't keep still. "What, Chuck?" I whispered. "What don't you know?"

When he turned to me, I saw a little boy's face, scared and sad and vulnerable. His eyes held so much pain, I almost had to look away.

"I don't know," he repeated slowly, "if God can ever forgive me for all that."

Anne Marie knelt beside him on the rough cement and gathered both his hands in hers. "Charles Summers, look at me." He obeyed. "There is nothing on this earth that God cannot forgive. Do you hear me? Nothing." She gave his hands a shake for emphasis. "Because of Jesus, Chuck, remember? Jesus paid the price for it when he died on the cross. Because of his sacrifice, you've already been forgiven."

My brother's eyes held hers for the longest time, then closed as he let his shoulders sag. No one moved. We must have looked like characters in a tableau when Jake came out and told me it was time to go.

As I stood to leave, I pulled Mama's letter from my pocket and placed it gently on my brother's lap.

Chapter
Thirty-six

I got so little sleep that night I had to force myself to go to church on Sunday morning. I couldn't get Chuck off my mind. Mama would have died all over again if she knew the state he'd gotten into. I knew he was still shaken, still confused. And the way we'd left it made me wonder if he accepted anything Anne Marie had said.

My meeting with Florence was only a few hours away, and I was as nervous as a schoolgirl on her first date. "What if she doesn't come?" I asked Jake. "She could just as easily change her mind and pack herself back to San Diego."

Jake just rolled his eyes and squeezed my hand. "She'll be there," he promised. But he was no more sure than I was.

We took our usual places in the pew next to Dotty and Sam. True to her word, Mary Margaret planted herself right behind Edna Livermore's left shoulder. Neither of the sisters noticed her until the pastor asked us to greet one another. By then it was too late for them to move.

Pastor Willis preached a sermon on the grace of God, and by the time he was finished there was hardly a dry eye in the sanctuary. At the altar call, four people went forward to accept Jesus as their Savior. I dared to peek. Mary Margaret stood firmly in her place with her head bowed like all the rest.

* * *

She was standing at the railing, watching the flamingos preen and dance. In her green shorts and halter top she looked more like a child than a twenty-one-year-old college student. Her hair had hung long and loose on Friday. Today it was gathered into a ponytail and tied with a bright yellow scarf.

I clutched Jake's arm and watched her. I tried to imagine her as our Baby Grace, all pink and pretty and smelling sweet, wrapped up in a soft blanket. But the memory was a fuzzy one at best.

Then she turned around. I heard Jake's soft intake of breath and felt my own heart pop. Would I ever get used to the resemblance? It could have been Krista standing there. Krista as I remembered her at seven, with her red-gold hair and button nose, a billion freckles marching across her face.

But Krista's eyes had been periwinkle blue to match my own and almost always bright with laughter. Florence's eyes flashed dark with fear and what I took to be a measure of defiance. She leaned for a moment against the railing; then, as if pulling the determination from somewhere inside that slender, little-girl body, she pushed away and strode purposefully toward the bench where Jake and I were standing.

She extended her hand in a formal greeting and looked somewhere over our shoulders, as if searching the crowd. To my relief, she didn't mention our meeting on campus. "Mrs. Freeman." Her voice quivered in spite of her effort to contain it. "Thanks for coming. I need . . . I mean, I had to talk to you."

Suddenly I saw her for what she was. Shy, frightened and confused by circumstances out of her control. Why, her whole identity was at stake. How would I feel if I found out after all these years that I was not Celia Summers but someone else entirely? I knew I would probably fight the idea, just as this girl had.

My own fears eased, then slid away entirely. My mouth curved in a smile. I took her small, trembling hand between both my own and led her to the bench behind us. Jake sat on the end, out of the way but watchful, still in awe of the resemblance that left no doubt. Florence DuVal or Elizabeth Grace Summers—whatever she chose to call herself, this girl was my sister. I knew it, Jake knew it, and so did she.

The crowd milled around us as we talked, offering more privacy than if there had been only a few people about. We were anonymous on this little bench at the entrance to one of the biggest zoos in the world. Her eyes and mine spilled tears, then laughter. I told her about her heritage, her short life as Baby Grace. She told me of her struggle to believe. I spoke of Mama and Papa, and showed her a picture of our other sister, Krista. "She died when she was seven," I said. "I still miss her."

Florence nodded. "I could see that when you looked at me." For the first time she glanced at Jake, then back to the picture. "I guess there's no mistaking it," she said, smiling through her tears. "We might as well be twins."

Jake disappeared for a time and returned with three bottles of Coke. We sipped them gratefully. She talked about her parents, how good they'd been to her, and her love for them. "I love Chuck too," she finally said. "He was always there for me. When I was little, I looked up to him. Adopted or not, he was my big brother. When we got older we were friends, but distant ones. He got into trouble a lot. I always thought it was just because he was a boy, you know? Fathers always expect more of their boys. Dad got after Chuck a lot. They had loud arguments at night sometimes, but I never knew what they were about." She grew quiet for a time, and I let her think.

"Until that night."

I was startled by her abrupt opening after the long silence, until I realized it was exactly what Chuck would have done.

"It was my fourteenth birthday. A boring party geared toward my mother's friends. Most of the boys went home early. Chuck took pity and danced with me. Then he told me all this stuff about our parents lying. He said I wasn't Florence at all. I was his sister Grace. His real sister. We had been adopted together."

She shook her head. "He'd said some of those things before, but this time was different. He was more forceful, more insistent. He . . . he scared me." She looked up at me, pleading with her eyes for understanding. I squeezed her hand and smiled encouragement. "I honestly thought he was making it up to get back at Mom and Dad. They hadn't been getting along at all.

"Like I said, he scared me and I lost it. Blew my cool. Started screaming and throwing things." She shuddered. "Then Daddy came and started yelling, and Chuck hit him. It was horrible."

She told the story like she was in a trance, with a flood of words I couldn't have stopped if I'd tried. "They told me Chuck was a hoodlum and a liar. They said he'd been involved with drugs that had damaged his brain. My father is a doctor. What was I supposed to believe? Anyway, they warned me not to see him or talk to him again. 'He's dangerous, Flo,' they said. 'You don't know what he might do or say. He's not your real brother, so stay away from him.' And I did, for a long time." She sighed. "I heard through the grapevine that he'd gone to Korea. He called me once when he got back, but we lost contact after that.

"When I heard about his accident, I went nuts. I wanted to visit him, but my father told me to stay away." Her mouth twisted in a grimace that I'd seen on Chuck's face many times in the last few months. "My father holds the purse strings, you know? It was either obey or lose my education. College isn't cheap, and I have no other source of income. At least, not yet."

Her face softened, and I thought about Jerry, the young man she'd been with in the cafeteria.

She took a deep breath. "You must think I'm hateful and vicious to not even care about my own brother. But I do, Mrs. Freeman."

"Celia."

"Celia. Chuck calls you Cissy." She tasted the name. "I care about Chuck, Celia. He's my brother, and I love him very much. I had to see you, meet you, and find out . . . How is he? I know he's not in the hospital; I got your letters. But how is he really?"

"I'm fine, Little Bit. Brother Chuck is doing fine."

I don't know who jumped the highest, Florence or me. He stood behind us on the other side of Jake, and neither of us had seen or heard him come. Florence had the better view. Her hand flew to her mouth, and her face turned gray beneath her freckles. I still don't know if it was his injuries or the shock of seeing him at all that held her frozen.

I thought Chuck might feel faint. He couldn't be on his feet very long, and I didn't know how long he'd been standing there with Anne hovering as unobtrusively as possible in the background.

I honestly don't know who made the first move. Florence let out a little cry, Chuck handed Jake his crutches, and before I could even blink she was in his arms. He held her gently, his free hand stroking her hair. It had come undone from the ponytail and hung loose around her shoulders. Anyone watching might have thought them lovers or lifelong friends.

The crowd around us surged by, oblivious to the scene. But for the rest of us, those of us who knew, it was like watching a happy dream unfold for real.

* * *

The meeting with Flo had gone well, but we were still up against their father's edict: she would not be allowed to visit with any of us openly. "He'll cut off my college fund for sure," she had whispered uneasily. And I had no doubt she was right.

She had declined Jake's invitation to drive her back to campus. "Thanks, but Jerry's waiting in the parking lot." She blushed and hugged her brother one more time. "Summer session is over, and we're heading back to San Diego today."

Brother and sister parted reluctantly. Florence shook hands with Jake and wrapped me in an awkward hug. "I'll be back in September. Somehow—well, maybe I can get Daddy to change his mind."

She hadn't looked very hopeful, and Chuck smirked. "Fat chance," he whispered as we watched our baby sister walk away. She was headed back to the only parents—the only life— she'd ever known.

Later, at Uncle Edward and Aunt Rose's house, Chuck told me it was Mama's letter that had made him come. "I read it at least six times," he said. "By the last time I finished it, I realized I wanted to forgive her." He shoved his hands deep into his pockets and studied the toes of his new black boots. "It won't be easy to forget it, sis; I can't promise that right now." He looked at me with tear-bright eyes, and I nodded my okay.

"A little at a time," Anne had said, and I knew she was right. It would take time for him to heal—not just physically, but emotionally and spiritually too.

"I also knew I still loved that kid sister of mine," Chuck went on. He grinned and flipped a lock of hair out of his eyes. "When Anne told me you were meeting Flo, I decided to give it one more try. Not just for Mama and the rest of you, but for me.

"I didn't think it would ever happen, but I feel more settled than I have in years, like I finally belong." He turned his face up toward the sky. "There's still a lot I don't understand. Maybe someday . . ." He shook his head and leaned heavily against the patio wall.

Chapter Thirty-six

We both knew it wasn't over. Uncle Edward had never pressed charges, of course, but there was still the matter of the stolen motorcycle. With the family's help, Chuck had been able to make full restitution for the ruined bike, but the police had judged the theft and the accident as having criminal intent; Chuck was scheduled to go to trial September 1.

I followed my brother's stare. Anne Marie was doing dishes at the kitchen sink, her head bent down, sunlight glinting on her silky brown hair.

Chuck never took his eyes off her. "I don't know where I'll go from here," he whispered, "but if this is a second chance at life, I'll take it."

I smiled but stayed quiet. His look was saying things I wasn't supposed to hear.

Epilogue

Mama's letter folded neatly along the creases and slipped glove-tight into the snap pocket on my handbag.

As I read, the goose was joined by his mate. Now they've drifted closer to the shoreline, just beneath the elms, to feed with the mallards.

Jake and Libby should be back soon. It cools off fast this time of year. The sun sets early, and Jake knows how I hate to travel the freeway after dark.

I've arranged to meet Florence for lunch tomorrow. We've visited twice since she came back to school. She's very sweet, really, but has a stubborn streak that reminds me of Papa. She's not as obstinate as Chuck, though. That boy hasn't got the sense God gave those geese. He's supposed to join us tomorrow, Flo and Jerry and me. I told Florence to ask Stuart Haley too. "The man has a head on his shoulders," I told her on the phone. "Maybe he can talk some sense into that brother of ours."

Chuck's court date turned out to be a hearing in a judge's chambers. The only other two people there were Uncle Edward and the artist from Long Beach. The policeman who had been at the accident scene was supposed to show up too, but it turned out he was serving as a witness at a jury trial and couldn't come.

That must have worked in Chuck's favor. That, and the fact that we'd already paid for the bike. He got off with sixty days of community service and six months on parole.

He'd been allowed to serve his sentence in San Bernardino, since he was staying with Aunt Rose and Uncle Edward. But now that he was feeling better and was through sweeping up nights at the county library, he was itchy as a hound with fleas. All he could talk about was moving into L.A. or up toward San Francisco.

"I can get a job anywhere slinging hash," he told Uncle Edward. "It might take a while, but I swear I'll pay you back."

It didn't matter that Aunt Rose cried and Uncle Edward told him, "Never mind. We don't want money, Chuck. You're family, and we're glad to have you as long as you want to stay."

But Chuck couldn't see it. Or he wouldn't. He refused to talk to his father either. "I don't need him, man. I can run my own life."

Even Anne Marie lost her patience with him. I don't know what was said, but she moved back to San Francisco two weeks ago and took a job at the hospital where she and Frank used to work. Everyone misses her sorely. Dave went around for a week threatening to "bust that guy's head open for messing with my sister," until Jake told him to button it or else he'd teach him a thing or two about busted heads. Neither Chuck nor Anne Marie will talk about it.

Mary Margaret's gone too. Quit her job at Douglas just like that. "I'm getting stale, Celia," she told me. "There's something better for me out there. Maybe I'll waitress for a while and go back to school. Wouldn't that just put a kink in everybody's chain?"

I don't know how she did it, but two days later she had a job as hostess at a restaurant in San Diego and enrolled herself as a four-year student at San Diego State. Her boyfriend, Michael, helped her move on Friday.

"Why can't people be content with what they have?" I asked Jake just last night. "We're always searching for something 'out there' just beyond our reach."

He laughed and pulled me closer to him on the couch. "Think what a dull world it would be if everyone stayed put, Cissy girl. And what about progress, like the new Salk polio vaccine and that transatlantic cable?" He smiled and kissed me on the chin. "Now me, I'm content right here at home. I have my wife and daughter and a growing business. What more could a man want?"

He does look happy strolling down the walkway from the zoo, toting a bottle of cola with two straws and wiping mustard off his chin. Libby has a flat white box: hot dogs and a carton of milk, I'll bet. Progress may be a good thing, but I have to admit I like this better: a roomy bench in a quiet park. A picnic supper with the ones I love.

And snow geese in the heart of Los Angeles on a November afternoon.